Where SUMMER *Never* COMES

Kristi Holl

Annie's®
AnniesFiction.com

Library of Congress-in-Publication Data
Where Summer Never Comes / by Kristi Holl
p. cm.
I. Title
                    2016945221

AnniesFiction.com
(800) 282-6643
Secrets of the Quilt™
Series Creator: Shari Lohner
Series Editors: Shari Lohner, Janice Tate, and Ken Tate
Cover Illustrator: Jonathan Bouw

10 11 12 13 14 | Printed in China | 9 8 7 6 5 4 3 2 1

1

Cabot Falls, Vermont
Present Day

Curled up on the couch in cropped pants and her favorite turquoise pullover, Sofia Parker pretended to be reading about silk quilts, but her churning stomach didn't match her calm demeanor. It should have been a peaceful Friday night. All four kids were home, watching a science-fiction movie in the family room. For once, Vanessa wasn't on a date, and the boys weren't gone with friends. No worries about anyone!

In theory, anyway.

Sofia sneaked another peek at her husband sitting in the next room at the dining table. For half an hour, he'd been alternating between running a hand through his thick blond hair and making frustrated sounds as he shuffled papers.

Was he studying the bank statement? Were they overdrawn? With skills that made him a great high school math teacher, he juggled their finances, and Sofia was glad he did. But she knew, with four children, it was a constant challenge to stretch his salary to cover their needs. Her catering business was growing, but it wasn't steady income yet.

When he rubbed the back of his neck and sighed again, Sofia could take it no longer.

"What's wrong?" she asked, winding a strand of light brown hair around her finger.

"Did you say something?"

Sofia deliberately kept the worry out of her voice. "Are we overdrawn?"

He tossed his reading glasses down on the table and turned around in his chair. "No, nothing like that." He rubbed his forehead. "I'm reviewing the printout of my midterm grades. Something didn't look right, so I'm comparing them with my grade book."

"And?"

"There are a few inconsistencies here, but I can't tell how they happened."

"What kind of inconsistencies?"

Before he could answer, Wynter bounded up the stairs from the basement. Tall for fifteen, she had long, wavy black hair that hid most signs of her cochlear implants.

"You guys have a minute?" She looked like a cat that got the cream. "I got my midterm grades today." She handed the report to Sofia. "Look."

Sofia read it eagerly. Wynter had been working overtime with daily tutoring to get caught up in her "hearing" classrooms. Sofia jumped up and hugged Wynter and handed the report to Jim. "Look at this! An A in biology! I had no idea you were doing so well."

"Me either, actually," Wynter admitted. "Last week Mr. Barton said I was getting a B-. I don't think I earned an A."

"What graded work have you done since then?" Jim asked.

"Just a frog dissection," Wynter said.

Sofia smiled. "Apparently the dissection was a big part of your grade."

Wynter shrugged, grabbed a bag of banana chips from the kitchen, and went back downstairs, but Jim continued to stare at her midterm report.

"Jim, what is it?" Sofia asked.

"Wynter didn't think she earned this grade," he said, reaching behind him for his printouts, "and I *know* that some of my students' math grades weren't earned either."

Sofia joined him at the table. "Show me," she said.

Jim pointed to his grade book, where grades were written in his precise hand, and then the corresponding printouts. Most of the grades matched up, but in three cases, grades that should have been Cs and Ds had magically been transformed into As and Bs.

"How in the world did this happen?" she asked.

"No idea." He stacked his papers and drained his coffee cup. "But I'm glad I spotted it before grades go out on Tuesday. Obviously there's been some computer error."

Sofia knew that for several years now, teachers had been entering their grades on password-protected websites accessed only on computers at school. "How did you happen to notice the changes?" she finally asked. "I would have missed them."

"I wanted to double-check my list of who qualified for the SHiPS program for help to get their grades up."

Sofia nodded. She loved the Special Helpers in Public Schools tutoring program. It had been a wonderful benefit for Wynter. The tutors in the program were mostly retired grandparents who donated their time and talents to tutor in a variety of subjects.

Sofia still didn't see why a simple mistake had upset her usually unflappable husband though. "Your grade mix-up is just a computer glitch, right?" she asked.

"I don't see how," Jim said. "And frankly, I'm suspicious about the students who are affected."

"What do you mean?"

"Nothing," Jim said quickly. "I'll get it straightened out. Don't worry about it."

Sofia nodded but watched her husband gather up the papers and his grade book before he left the room. She knew him, and for some reason, Mr. Calm was worrying enough for both of them.

With a few minutes to herself, Sofia resumed her research. She was trying to decipher the origin of the eleventh block of a priceless silk patchwork quilt she'd inherited from Elena "Nonna" Baresi, her beloved Italian grandmother. Lately, Sofia's catering business had occupied the little time her family didn't require. But earlier in the month, her older sisters, Rosa and Gina, had asked rather pointedly when she planned to finish the last two squares.

Each of twelve different blocks in the quilt was of historical significance—at least, according to Nonna. To Sofia's great surprise, she'd been entrusted with the quest of discovering which distinguished ancestor had pieced each square and how it had come to be in the quilt. A leather-bound diary written in Italian had accompanied the quilt, and Nonna claimed it contained enough clues to find the answers.

Fergus, their border collie, trotted in and came to lay his head on Sofia's knee. She patted him absentmindedly, knowing he was reminding her that it was past the kids' bedtime and his too. Sofia empathized with their collie. He didn't like his routine disturbed any more than Sofia did, and like her, Fergus didn't rest until everyone was tucked in.

"Go play for a bit, Fergus," she said, shifting her legs. "You're shedding on my book."

The eleventh silk block was quite dainty, even fragile, in appearance. It had been pieced from a light lavender paisley print, with a darker lavender featherstitch added. Her fabric research showed that the paisley print came from the right time period, but she had no idea what country it had originated from. It could have been Italy, but her research showed that it also could have come from Persia, India, Russia, the United States, Paris, England, or Scotland. *Paisley* was the term given to the pattern of curving shapes found on silk and cotton fabrics. It had always reminded Sofia of teardrops.

Sofia stretched her tired back, rolled her neck from side to side, then settled back in for her favorite part—the leather diary of clues written in Italian. While Sofia had struggled with the translations in the beginning, her Italian had come back to her as she'd worked to decipher the intriguing entries. She rarely even needed her online translator anymore. Feet curled under her and notebook at hand, she opened the diary and read.

As she translated, she copied the words in her notebook. Since paisley print had been made in so many countries, she needed to keep an open mind.

Some words were no surprise: the Italian words for "paisley," "silk," and "quilt." However, this particular diary entry was more difficult to read than previous ones. One corner of the writing had faded, and several words were blurred, as if a tear or water droplet had fallen there long ago. Using a magnifying glass, Sofia held the diary directly under the lamp and peered more closely. The most smeared word looked like "*mor*" or "*moro*" to her. The last words were more clear; "Gia" was short for "Gianna," she knew, which was Italian for "Jane." And "Carlotta" was "Charlotte" in English.

Fergus returned, and Sofia absently stroked his head. He snuffled and shifted. *I think he would purr if he could.* She let the translated Italian words roll around in her head. As she did, excitement began to bubble up.

Jane. Paisley. Moor. Quilt. Charlotte.

Stay calm, she told herself sternly, *and don't jump to conclusions.*

As much as she loved British authors, she knew there was virtually no chance that her paisley quilt square had come from Charlotte Brontë, the author who lived on the moors of northern England where she wrote *Jane Eyre*.

All weekend the tension grew, and Sofia's inner spring wound tighter. Jim had grown quieter, and when she asked what he believed had happened to his grades, he was evasive and then changed the subject.

That wasn't at all like the Jim Parker she knew.

Why was he so concerned? Couldn't he just correct the mistakes made by the computer and be done with it?

"I'm going to school tonight," he said after Sunday's pizza supper, "and fix whatever happened with the grades. I know which students need SHiPS help, but if their grades don't show that they need tutoring, they'll get passed over."

"How will you get in?" Sofia asked.

"I called the principal, and Ed said he'd be around tonight for that community concert and talent show they're doing to raise money for the senior trip. And if I can't find him, I'll ask the janitor to let me into the school. He'll be there to clean up afterward."

"I'll come with you." Sofia nodded at the line of miniature white cakes lined up to cool on racks on the kitchen counter. "Then I could set up for tomorrow's first class tonight."

"Are you nervous about teaching?"

"Yes and no." Sofia had become quite well known after catering two high-profile weddings. Last Christmas, she'd provided cake for the wedding of the daughter of the home economics teacher, April Fielding. Because of that, Mrs. Fielding had invited her to demonstrate her cake decorating skills to her four general classes and one advanced cooking class at the high school. One week she'd teach cake decorating, and the second week she planned candy-making classes. She'd be paid a substitute teacher's wages. She would have done it for free, but the extra income was appreciated.

"You kids finish your homework while we're gone, and no TV." Sofia picked up her basket containing her pastry bags, metal decorating tips, offset spatulas, and food coloring. "Vanessa, you're in charge. I'll check homework when we get back in an hour."

At seventeen, their petite blonde looked frail, but looks were deceiving. "Aye aye, Captain!" she said, giving a salute.

After Jim helped Sofia load the Suburban with her dozen carefully wrapped mini cakes, they drove in silence to the high school. The custodian let them in with his pass key, and Sofia was grateful for Jim's help carrying the cakes to the home ec kitchen in the basement.

"It's peaceful and quiet on the weekends," Jim said. "During the day, you can hardly hear yourself think." He smiled. "You'll see tomorrow."

"I'm looking forward to it." At his raised eyebrow, she grinned and added, "Well, mostly."

"You'll do great," Jim said. "If I didn't have to teach tomorrow, I'd come decorate a cake too, just to see the pretty teacher."

"Oh, ha," she said. "You'd come for the cake."

"Well, that too." He gave her a quick kiss. "I'll be upstairs in my room. Come up after you set up your stations."

"Will do."

Sofia wondered how it would feel to be the real teacher, to take charge of the classroom every day. It would be overwhelming, she thought, but for two weeks, it sounded like fun to show students some tricks of the trade. She'd added a small line of homemade candies that had been a hit at both weddings, and she knew the girls would enjoy making some. She wondered briefly if the classes would be all girls or if some budding male chefs would be there too.

In just twenty minutes, she had set up the eight stations with a mini cake and decorating utensils at each place. She'd show them how to make frosting stiff enough to decorate with, then give them eighteen-point star tips for their practicing. The same tip could make star flowers, a reverse shell border, and rosettes. She hoped students arrived on time, because she'd need every minute to accomplish what she planned.

Taking one last glance around, Sofia shut off the lights, then pulled the door closed and tested to make sure that it automatically locked.

Jim had turned the lights on in the hallways, but even so, the school was a bit spooky as her footsteps echoed in the quiet building.

At the far northwest corner, she started up the stairwell to the third floor and Jim's math room. She climbed up a floor, turned, and climbed again. As she opened the door at the top floor, a dark form rushed at her, slamming into her with a grunt.

Flying backward, Sofia clutched frantically for the railing to avoid being thrown down the stairs. Someone in a dark hoodie and black high-tops stepped over her and raced down the stairs two at a time.

Stunned, Sofia rolled over on her hands and knees, took a gasping breath, and dragged herself to her feet. She shook her head to clear it.

And then it hit her.

Jim!

His math classroom was just two doors down. Had the person who'd slammed into her also attacked Jim?

Barely breathing, she ran down the hall and yanked the doorknob of Jim's math room. She twisted it and pushed, but the door wouldn't budge.

"Jim! Open the door!"

Sofia pressed her nose against the vertical panel of glass in the door, trying to see into the half-darkened room. She knew Jim's desk was at the back, hidden from sight behind a tall metal storage cabinet.

"Jim! Are you in there? Open the door!"

She searched up and down the empty hallway. Was Jim even in his classroom? Maybe she should go look for him—or call the police.

Then she heard it: a groan.

"Jim, it's me! Sofia!" She pounded again and pressed her face to the glass.

Down on the floor, Jim was crawling forward from behind the cabinet. Blood ran down one side of his face. He looked up once, then fell to the floor and lay still.

Heart pounding so hard that her hands shook, Sofia grabbed her phone and dialed 911.

2

Yorkshire, England
July 1848

*C*harlotte Brontë slapped her copy of a London newspaper down on the train seat beside her. "How could the newspaper allow such a scathing review of *Jane Eyre*?"

"What does it say?" Her younger sister Anne bounced in the carriage seat opposite her.

Charlotte snatched the paper back up. "Listen to this: 'Despite *Jane Eyre* selling in astounding numbers, we must warn women readers of its raw passions and unseemly behavior of the heroine. In fact, women should not be allowed to read it!'"

She fanned herself, hot despite the early morning hour. The droplight window in the carriage door was down, but it brought in more soot than cool air. It didn't really matter anyway, as her internal temperature was close to the boiling point.

Anne nervously pleated her burgundy-colored skirt. The pink ribbons of her poke bonnet fluttered in the breeze from the window. "If readers think *Jane Eyre* is full of raw passion, how much more criticism there will be if the public discovers that a *woman* wrote it!" Her tan freckles stood out against her pale skin.

"And an unmarried clergyman's daughter at that," Charlotte added.

Jane Eyre had been published the previous year, the same year as their sister Emily's novel, *Wuthering Heights*. Anne's most recent novel was *The Tenant of Wildfell Hall.* They'd published under the male pseudonyms of Currer, Ellis, and Acton Bell. Even their publishers had had no idea that the authors were women. At least, not until this overwhelming and exhausting trip to London.

"I'm sorry the review was so harsh," Anne said.

"It was mild compared to this column: 'No real woman would create a character as unseemly as *Jane Eyre.* The character of Jane has no attractive, feminine qualities.'"

Anne waved a gloved hand before her face, as if to dispel a foul odor. "Read something else to me. Let's forget their unkind words."

Charlotte turned the pages. "'Robbers managed to steal a shipment of gold from a sealed baggage railroad car on a train moving more than fifty miles per hour. It happened in broad daylight.'"

"Oh, Charlotte!" Anne twisted her fingers together in her lap. "Papa warned us not to travel by train, just two ladies alone. Why did we ever leave the safety of the parsonage?"

"You know why," Charlotte said. Speculation in the press about their novels had forced the sisters to go in person to London to prove their identities to their publishers.

"At least the editors at Smith, Elder, and Company promised to keep our secret," Anne said.

"I'm sure they'll guard our privacy," Charlotte agreed.

Anne shuddered. "The mere *thought* of strangers knowing who we are and showing up on our doorstep to gawk at us . . ."

Charlotte understood. She, too, was revolted by the idea of people thinking they had the right to pry into their lives. Their father, in his seventies, wouldn't cope well either. She reached across the rocking train carriage to grip her sister's slender hand. "I promise that won't happen. Coming with me to prove we are two women is all I needed from you. We'll be back in Haworth today, safe from prying eyes."

Charlotte's dream was the same as her sisters'. They desperately wanted to be left alone to write, to make necessary income at home without having to teach or be governesses again. Charlotte was never happier than when home with her sisters, brother, and father. Even with her brother so ill, they were a contented family. As the train rounded a steep curve, she rocked sideways and bumped her shoulder. First class or not, the Great Northern Railway carriages were more like riding in a stagecoach.

Anne laid a small hand at her throat. "Let us not talk about this distressing subject any longer. It's behind us now." Her eyes sparkled then. "Let us discuss the opera we saw! Emily won't believe we saw *The Barber of Seville* at the Theatre Royal in Covent Garden."

"But how dowdy we looked." Charlotte rolled her eyes. "There we were, in our plain travel clothes, when Mr. Smith arrived wearing tails. I was mortified next to the ladies in their elegant dresses and expensive jewelry." As usual when under stress, she'd come down with a bilious attack and severe headache. "But I'm truly happy that you enjoyed it, Anne. I know light opera is your favorite." Her younger sister regularly bought sheet music and attended recitals when she could.

Charlotte peered out the window as the train approached the Derby station. "I wish trains had lavatories onboard," she said.

Anne laughed. "That will never happen."

"Are you getting out? We have fifteen minutes till it pulls out again."

"Yes." Anne grabbed her hand luggage and slipped her reticule over her wrist. She carried her lightweight crocheted shawl over the other arm. Already the summer morning was too hot for it.

As Charlotte stepped out of the carriage, people poured out up and down the platform. Tall hats on dark-coated gentlemen bobbed like corks, while ladies in restrictive corsets dared not exert themselves for fear of fainting. Next door, a stout woman with well-groomed gray hair emerged. A slim young woman, her upper arms skeletal in their tight sleeves, leaned on the older woman. Charlotte glanced north and spotted the booking office and waiting rooms. To the south she was thankful to see the lavatory.

Charlotte kept a sharp eye for thieves and pickpockets as they hurried along. The lavatory was full when they arrived, and they waited outside in the shade. Charlotte watched passersby and noted the two ladies from first class approaching.

The older woman glided toward them like a steamship heading into port, her dress with its bell-shaped skirt lavishly trimmed with frills, lace, braid, fringe, and ribbons. With her numerous heavy petticoats and tightly laced whalebone corset, Charlotte doubted she could draw a deep breath. Her ensemble was enveloped in a black lace mantilla.

As they drew nearer, Charlotte realized the younger woman wasn't just slender, she was ailing. Charlotte's eyes narrowed. Seriously ill. And yet, when the auburn-haired girl caught Charlotte's eyes, she smiled brightly. She was impeccably dressed, and the dark-green lace scarf tucked into the neckline of her paler green dress was the exact color of her eyes. Despite the heat of the July morning, she was wrapped in a lavender paisley shawl. While she didn't appear to be more than eighteen or nineteen, fine lines made a delicate web on her forehead and a crease between her eyebrows. Charlotte recognized the signs. This young woman was often in pain.

Charlotte nodded to her. "Would you like to go ahead of us? You appear unwell."

The older woman pushed ahead of Charlotte and Anne. "My daughter has nervous prostration."

The girl rolled her eyes heavenward and then quickly resumed her placid expression.

"I'm sorry to hear that!" Anne said. "That can be debilitating in its exhaustion."

"I'm quite fine—"

"No, Mary, you are not!" Her mother lifted her head high, then looked down her nose at the Brontë sisters' plain clothes and worn hand luggage. Charlotte studied her face in amusement as the woman's need to impress struggled with her hesitancy to mingle with the less wealthy. Impressing them won out. "My daughter is being attended to by a famous London physician. Surely you've heard of him. Dr. Lydgate. We've just seen him."

"Mother worries too—"

"And along with her medicine, he recommends profound quiet and extended vacations to the countryside."

"The extended vacation sounds lovely," Charlotte said. "I hope you find it restorative."

Mary fingered the cameo brooch pinned to her scarf. "I do believe—"

"We'll retire to our country home the moment her father returns from France." Mary's mother paused, eyebrow lifted, as if expecting exclamations or eager questions. When the Brontë sisters were silent, she went on. "My husband, Mr. Green, is attending a banking conference in Paris. He runs the Bank of England branch in Leeds."

The young girl winced and seemed to fold in on herself, but whether from pain or embarrassment, Charlotte couldn't tell.

The lavatory attendant opened the door then and stepped aside while two women emerged. Two ladies ahead of the Greens went inside.

Charlotte knew the Leeds train station, being a connecting

point to many of the places she visited. She turned to the girl. "Do you like Leeds?"

The young woman smiled. "Yes, I do. I help with a group of children—"

Mrs. Green's strident voice overpowered Mary's. "Because of my work with the Band of Hope—I'm chairman of our temperance society—my daughter is allowed to work with the children. But it has tired her, and she must stop and get well."

"No!" With difficulty, Mary visibly swallowed the rest of her outburst. "Forgive me. If you believe it's necessary—"

"I do. Dr. Lydgate prescribed complete rest."

"Yes, Mother." Her controlled voice was subdued, but Charlotte noted the bright-red spots on Mary's cheeks and how her fingers curled tightly into a fist.

The pause was awkward until Anne turned to Mrs. Green. "I admire your work with the Band of Hope. Men—and children— must be warned of the health dangers of drink." Charlotte agreed, knowing Anne was thinking of their brother Branwell's trouble with alcohol. It had made him gravely ill.

Mrs. Green preened herself like a peacock. "Last August, we had Mrs. Ann Jane Carlile to speak to our local women and schoolchildren. So many men and youth signed the pledge against drinking! In November, we held our first official local chapter meeting in Leeds."

Just then, the lavatory attendant motioned for the Greens to enter, and soon, it was the Brontës' turn. When outside again, they hurried back to their train compartment, passing the coach where the Greens were already comfortably situated. Charlotte caught a glimpse of Mary Green, and the young girl's expression reminded her for all the world of a trapped rabbit's.

One blue-uniformed guard was seated on top of their carriage already, and a second guard punched their train tickets. *He must be a slacker,* Charlotte thought, noting his spotless uniform as he hurried toward the guard car at the end of the first-class carriages.

"Hurry up, Charlotte," Anne called, "and stop staring."

Charlotte climbed into the carriage. It was true. She couldn't stop herself from people watching. It was her writer's nature. "Collecting characters," Anne called it. "Being nosy," their clergyman father said.

It was only a ten-minute ride to the next station, so Charlotte left her book in her bag. Staring out the window at the passing countryside, she marveled at the beautiful scenery. She truly loved the desolate moors at Haworth, but these rolling green hills dotted with sheep and stone fences were soothing after the tumult of London. The train maintained a steady speed through open country. From time to time, they overtook carts rumbling along dirt roads running parallel with the tracks.

They pulled into the Sheffield station, jerking to a halt with a massive hiss of steam. Only two people waited at the platform, but there would be more before the train left in thirty minutes. One young woman with clusters of blond curls falling over her ears stepped toward the Greens' carriage in front of them. The blonde's rose-colored skirt had three tiers of flounces, gathered tightly at the top and stiffened with horsehair braid at the bottom.

"Look!" Charlotte pointed at her. "Her dress has short sleeves!"

"In the daytime?" Anne gasped and leaned near the window to stare. "And the neck!"

The neckline wasn't particularly low, nor was the gown off the shoulders like evening wear, but it was extremely daring for daytime. Charlotte privately named her Miss Oo-La-La.

"How audacious!" Anne said.

"True," Charlotte said, fanning herself, "but in such heat, I'd gladly wear short sleeves and fewer petticoats if I could get away with it."

A moment after the blonde disappeared inside the Greens' carriage, Mary Green appeared alone and walked away toward the vendor.

"I'm going to stretch my legs," Charlotte said. "Will you accompany me?"

"No. I will stay and watch our luggage." Anne pulled the knitting from her bag and continued work on the black worsted wool muffler she was making for Father.

Charlotte followed Mary, nodding to Mrs. Green as she passed. Mrs. Green scowled in obvious disdain at the newcomer to her carriage, and Charlotte stifled a laugh. A moment later, she caught up with Mary, who sat on a bench.

"May I join you?" Charlotte asked. "Or can I get you some tea from the vendor? or a tea cake?"

"Thank you, no, but I welcome your company."

Charlotte made herself comfortable. "I was admiring your beautiful shawl earlier," Charlotte said. "The color reminds me of the heather that I love."

"I would judge that this lavender would look better with your coloring," Mary said. "I've grown so pale and washed out."

Another train steamed into the station in a riot of noise, vibration, and pungent smoke. After passengers alighted, a porter climbed onto the roof of the first carriage and passed down the luggage to another porter. Stacked on the platform, it was soon claimed by various owners and then carried away for them.

Angling her head slightly to see around her bonnet's broad rim, Charlotte watched Mary out of the corner of her eye. The girl gradually slumped as much as a corset would allow, but when Charlotte turned to her, she quickly straightened, pulling her paisley shawl tighter. She looked to Charlotte like someone who needed a friend.

"Nervous prostration sounds like a difficult disease to cure," Charlotte began.

Mary snorted. "The doctor is a ninny." She shook her head. "He said I contracted it by an 'intemperate exercise of the intellectual faculties.'"

Charlotte had to laugh. It was a wonder she and her sisters didn't have nervous prostration then, after writing so much!

Mary licked her lips. "His medicine only makes me feel worse. My vision gets blurry, like things are in a mist. The lethargy, the sleepiness, is the worst."

Charlotte's heart sank. Did she dare mention that she recognized the signs of too much laudanum use? She knew doctors prescribed it for everything from nerves to babies teething, but she also knew it could have devastating effects. She firmly believed it had caused Branwell's problems to worsen. "Do you have to take it?" Charlotte asked.

"Yes, but I take less than Mama thinks. But when Mama is watching me—like today—she makes sure I swallow every drop of the tonic." She smiled. "I've been excited lately, but I'm not high-strung, no matter what Mama says."

"Excited?" Charlotte asked. "Something good, I hope."

Mary lowered her voice. "Yes, but if Mama knew my plans, she'd lock me in the attic and never let me out."

Charlotte tried to draw Mary out further, but it quickly became apparent that the girl regretted sharing her feelings so openly.

"Well," Charlotte finally said, "I hope you feel well soon."

They fell silent, and Charlotte studied her surroundings. It was a busy morning. Freight trains thundered past in both directions on the through lines in the middle. Another short train flew by, comprising an empty first-class carriage, a bright-red mail coach, and a guard's van. Their own train remained where it had stopped. The Great Northern engine, painted green with a black smoke box and chimney, gleamed in the morning sun.

She had often watched her father studying the steam engines, while Charlotte contented herself making mental notes about the people strolling on the platform. There was the thin, bony-faced young man with the prominent chin and curved shoulders. She guessed *Mr. Chin* spent his time hunched over a workbench. Another young man ambled along, his soft hat, old spectacles, and leather satchel making him look bookish. *Mr. Studious,* Charlotte thought. Strutting past her was a heavy older man, pulling back one side of his coat to show his velvet suspenders with silk embroidery. His fluffy sideburns, extending to the corners of his mouth, blew in the breeze. *Mr. Muttonchops.* He passed close to, but ignored, a constable. The policeman had overly large canines, giving him a snarling look even when he smiled. *Constable Mad Dog,* Charlotte decided.

Charlotte glanced at Mary, whose shoulders drooped again. "I'm getting you some tea, with lots of sugar," she said. Overriding Mary's protests, she headed toward the vendor.

On the way back with the tea, Charlotte kicked something with her foot. Kneeling carefully, she grabbed a blue cap with a hard visor from where it was half hidden by her skirt. A guard's cap! And a long, wavy, reddish hair was stuck inside it. Charlotte smiled. One of the guards had a secret lady friend—or maybe just a wife with wavy hair who brushed his cap. She glanced around but didn't see anyone missing his cap. She laid it on an unoccupied bench and moved on.

Charlotte coaxed Mary to drink the sugary tea, but Mary's hand trembled so much that she set the cup down before spilling it.

"Can I help you back to your carriage?" Charlotte asked, fearing that the weak-looking girl might faint.

"In a moment." Mary closed her eyes and leaned back, letting the sun hit her face.

Charlotte waited, wondering if she should fetch Mrs. Green.

Suddenly, a shadow covered them. "Can I help you, miss?" asked a young guard with horn-rimmed glasses. "Are you unwell?" He was in his twenties, and Charlotte thought his thin mustache needed fertilizer.

Mary sat forward, flustered. "No no, I'm fine." She glanced up at the young man, blushed, and gripped her hands together in her lap. "Truly."

His pronounced Adam's apple went up and down as he swallowed, and he looked genuinely worried.

"Well. . ." He slipped the metal handle of his signal lamp over his arm. "I'll be going then." He moved away but twice glanced back over his shoulder.

Mary watched him until he disappeared into the guard van, a half-wistful expression on her thin face. "Wasn't he kind?"

"I think he admired you," Charlotte said.

Mary studied Charlotte's face, opened her mouth, closed it again, and pressed her lips together. "I actually *do* have an admirer," she finally said. "But Mama and Papa would never think him appropriate for me."

Charlotte frowned. She'd experienced unrequited love years ago, and she knew it was a ticket to heartbreak. "Is your admirer . . . married?"

"Of course not!" Mary lowered her voice. "But my parents would think he is beneath the daughter of a wealthy banker."

"So they've never met him?"

"They have no idea he even exists."

"How is that possible?" Charlotte asked. "Your mother keeps such careful watch over you. How could you have an admirer without her knowing?"

"We met through Band of Hope. Several of us took a group of children on an outing to Blackpool. The children loved seeing the seaside for the first time. My admirer brought some children from London. I watched him and loved how he treated the boys in his charge. When the Band of Hope organization later arranged an excursion to Scarborough, we had an opportunity to talk. The more we talked, the more I admired him."

Charlotte raised one eyebrow. "Where was Mrs. Green during that excursion?"

"Mama was sick and stayed home at the last minute. She didn't want me to go without her, but the children were counting on me. Some were as young as six. There were other adults along too." She sighed. "Mama thinks I wore myself out with the children. It is true I was busy, but I loved it. I've also helped with bazaars. Once, I even hired a magic lantern slide show for them."

"They must have loved that!"

A blush slowly spread up Mary's neck. "I took a group to a music competition in London a few months ago. Mama had another obligation that day. I got to know him much better there. His group also sang in the competition." She leaned closer to Charlotte and lowered her voice. "We got our picture in the London newspaper together with our children. He sent me the picture." She sighed. "Mama would never let me have his letters if she saw them first, but our housekeeper sorts the mail." She patted the side of her skirt. "I keep them with me, in a secret pocket."

Charlotte could understand that. She would hate for her family to read her private letters too.

Mary twisted her fingers together. "If Mama ever found my letters, she'd *kill* me."

Charlotte hid her smile. Oh, the drama and passion of the young.

"We'd better get onboard now," Charlotte said. "They've

loaded the coal." She stood and gave the young woman her arm. "I hope good things for you and your admirer."

On the next segment of the journey, from Sheffield to Leeds, where the Greens lived, Charlotte settled back into a corner of her upholstered seat and closed her eyes. They'd returned late from the opera the night before and then rose before dawn to make it to the London station.

She tried to relax, but it was a noisy journey. The chugging of the locomotive combined with the rattling of the carriages and the clicking of the wheels on the rails produced a discordant racket. The carriage lurched from side to side as the train powered its way down the tracks.

Charlotte gave up. Reading would make her drowsy, but the jouncing of the train kept her awake. She stared out the window, noting where they had been since she was in the seat facing backward. The scenery blurred at the speed they traveled, adding to her sleepiness.

Suddenly, something small and dark flew into the ditch. Was it luggage from the roof? or something tossed from the first-class carriage right behind them? She leaned near the open window to see as, without warning, the train went dark for a few moments as it passed through a short tunnel under a stone bridge.

A minute later, Charlotte gathered her belongings as they pulled into the Leeds station. Made of limestone, the station had a lattice footbridge at the north end that spanned the platforms.

With a black belch of smoke, their train screeched to a halt. Charlotte stepped out and stretched her tired back as she watched people pour from the carriages. Just ahead was Mrs. Green. She unfolded her parasol's carriage handle and searched the platform, then marched over to a porter. "Where is my manservant?" she demanded. "He's supposed to be meeting our train. Help me find him!"

Charlotte chuckled at the porter's annoyed expression. Mary Green wasn't the only one who found her mother overbearing.

Next, Miss Oo-La-La, the lady with the shockingly short sleeves, stepped down. She strutted and swayed toward the rear of the train. Charlotte bet she was heading to the guard car to claim a larger piece of luggage. She looked like a woman who traveled with plenty of clothes.

While Mrs. Green bossed the porter around, Charlotte stepped over to their carriage to say goodbye to Mary. But she was dozing, her lavender paisley shawl draped over the back of the seat. Charlotte backed away quietly, stepping on some broken glass and grinding it under her foot. She glanced down, disgusted by the smell of liquor. Why did travelers have to carry such refreshment on the trains? She spotted a guard and went to inform him of the broken glass that needed clearing away.

Anne was still waiting for her when she got back to their carriage.

"Shall we go over?" Charlotte asked. She gripped her travel bag by its sturdy handle, hooked her hand through Anne's arm, and set off for the footbridge. Their connecting train didn't leave for another half hour, but they needed to change platforms. The Leeds platforms were covered by an overall low-pitched timber roof with alternate panels of off-white and light-purple glass. They crossed over several sets of tracks, then came back down a flight of wooden stairs to the platform on the other side. Once they caught their train to Keighley, they'd be nearly home, with just a walk from the Keighley station to the parsonage at Haworth.

Charlotte settled herself on a bench, found her place in her book, and began to read. Suddenly, the air was filled with one heartrending cry after another.

Charlotte stared at Anne, whose openmouthed expression

matched her own horror, for the terrified screams sounded like Mrs. Green.

"Mary's dead!" Her words echoed across the tracks. "My daughter's been murdered!"

3

Cabot Falls, Vermont
Present Day

$\mathcal{S}$ofia stumbled over her words as she gave information to the dispatcher, then put her on speakerphone and shouted at Jim again. Before the first responders arrived, Jim regained consciousness and sat up, dazed. Then, hand on his bleeding head, he stumbled to the door and unlocked it.

"Are you all right?" Sofia asked, pulling her husband's handkerchief from his pocket and pressing it against his head. "What happened?"

"Intruder," Jim said, collapsing in a chair. "Took me by surprise by my desk."

Five minutes later, Sofia's phone gave a call-waiting beep. She kept the dispatcher on the line while she answered it.

"The EMTs called me," Officer Ryan Quimby said. "We're at the front door. Can you come down and let us in?"

Sofia was reluctant to leave Jim, but she was relieved to see an officer she knew and trusted when she opened the locked door. The next two hours passed in a haze. Sofia called Vanessa from the ambulance, then followed up with updates from the ER, where Jim received three stitches in his head.

After the doctors were sure Jim had no concussion, Officer Quimby questioned them. "So you didn't recognize the intruder?" he asked. "Man or woman, boy or girl? A student maybe?"

"I never saw the person's face," Jim admitted. "I unlocked my room and turned on the light, but then I went to use the restroom. I came back and headed straight to my desk." He shrugged. "When I walked around the tall cabinet at the back, I got clobbered." He shook his head ruefully, then groaned a bit. "I didn't know what hit me."

The officer made quick notes. "The intruder must have entered your classroom while you were down the hall."

"I was knocked down by someone in a hoodie in the stairwell," Sofia said.

"Description?"

She thought back. "I had the impression that it was a young man, but I don't really know. Hoodie, jeans, sneakers . . . could have been a girl, I guess."

"I do know one thing," Jim said. "My laptop wasn't taken. Neither was the test that lay next to my computer."

Officer Quimby closed his notebook. "Your intruder either wasn't after your computer, or you interrupted him—or her—in the act, and the intruder panicked."

"Either way," Sofia said, "you're not going to school tomorrow."

Jim protested, but Sofia was firm. Now that the crisis had passed, she was weak in the knees with relief. She could have lost Jim that night. Tomorrow, he'd stay in bed even if she had to hog-tie him to it.

Throughout Monday, Sofia enjoyed teaching cake decorating to the home economics classes. April Fielding dressed in her apron that proclaimed, *Where there's a whisk, there's a way,*

watched Sofia's demonstrations eagerly. Mrs. Fielding brought photos of her daughter's wedding to show her students what Sofia had created.

But even as Sofia demonstrated how to make stars and rosettes, a part of her mind was tormented by the attack on Jim. She hoped he was staying in bed, but she highly doubted it.

After school, when she'd finished washing the icing bowls and tools, she walked out into the hallway and was shocked to see Vanessa there—with Jim.

"What are you doing here?" she demanded. "And how did you get to school?"

"Dad called me during PE," Vanessa said. "He told me to come home and bring him to school to talk to Principal Piper. I borrowed the Suburban . . ."

Sofia bit back angry words and glared at them both. "If he'd asked *me* to come get him, I would have said no."

Jim smiled. "That's why I didn't call you."

Hands in the air, Vanessa was backing down the hall. "I'm not getting caught in the middle," she said. "I'm off to play rehearsal."

"And I'm off to the office to talk to Ed about my school insurance and lesson plans for my sub. Won't take long."

Sofia fell into step with her husband. "I'll come too and drive you home," she said firmly. Upstairs and past the front double doors, they stepped into the principal's outer office.

"Hi, Madge," Jim said.

The school secretary, her hair in tight gray curls and glasses hanging on a chain, made *tsk-tsk*-ing noises at Jim's bandage. "Mr. Piper is waiting for you. Lance Barton will be meeting with you as well."

Sofia raised an eyebrow. What was the science teacher doing at their meeting? Surely he wasn't substituting in Jim's math classes.

Taking a straight-backed chair next to the secretary's desk, Sofia felt like a naughty student called to the principal's office. Within a minute, a phone call took Madge off to see the guidance counselor about a truant student.

Sofia closed her eyes, suddenly aware of how extraordinarily weary she was. She hadn't slept more than a couple of hours the night before. Her adrenaline rush had left her wired, and Jim's head injury made her afraid to fall asleep. She checked continually to be sure he was breathing.

Shuffling footsteps made her sit up straight. "Oh, hello, Mr. Jeffries."

"Nice to see you, Mrs. Parker." The elderly gentleman glanced at the secretary's desk. "Is Miss Bender around? I need to check my schedule for tomorrow."

"She just stepped out," Sofia said. "Did you have a nice weekend?"

"Yes, thank you." He checked his watch. "My grandson and I saw the movie uptown last night."

Sofia smiled. She admired Stephen Jeffries so much. His grandson, Adam, was a senior and had lived with him for many years. Sofia wasn't sure what had happened to Adam's parents. He worked on the school play with Vanessa, and she liked him.

"While you're here, Mr. Jeffries, let me thank you for all the help you've given Wynter this quarter. Her grades have improved, thanks to you."

"You're so welcome," Mr. Jeffries said. "Not every student assigned to us appreciates it. Students like her make me love the SHiPS program."

Just then, an angry voice erupted from behind the principal's closed door.

"How dare you insinuate that I'm fixing grades?" the science teacher demanded. Principal Piper's voice was quieter and calmer, but Lance Barton interrupted. "You're actually asking how we can afford a new home on my salary?" Another murmured question brought an even angrier response. "No, I won't tell you where we got the money. What is this? I've taught here for twenty years! I'm contacting the union rep!"

Mr. Jeffries cleared his throat nervously and backed out of the office. "I'll come back another time."

But Sofia barely noticed him leave. All the voices were raised now. From the sounds of it, Jim and the science teacher were being accused of grade fixing! *Is that why Wynter got an A in biology?* Sofia strained to hear the principal's softer words.

"This is grounds for firing and even for prosecution," Piper said. "We've got to get to the bottom of it, and I need your cooperation. The sooner we have answers, the sooner things will get back to normal."

Voices dropped then, and Sofia missed some of what was said, but she knew Jim's voice. "And for what reason?" she heard him say.

"We cross-checked grades of certain students we have been tracking. Several athletes had their grades changed in algebra, and now they'll be able to go to state this spring."

"But why would I do that, Ed?" Jim said. "I have no vested interest in the athletic program."

A long silence followed, and Sofia tried to calm her pounding heart so she could hear the principal's response.

"A teacher looks better when his or her students get higher grades. There have been cases when teachers were paid by the parents to change grades. Some of these kids' parents have money." He paused. "It was also suggested that you exchanged favors to get higher grades for your daughter Wynter."

Sofia gasped. Wynter *had* told them she didn't earn that A in biology.

"I hate to do this," Ed Piper said, sounding truly sorry, "but you're both suspended until we find out what has happened."

"But what about the intruder in my room last night?" Jim asked.

"You said nothing was taken and that your computer wasn't on."

"Maybe I interrupted the hacker before he could do anything. He was in there for some reason!"

"The police are looking into it. We'll do all we can to avoid a scandal. That wouldn't be helpful to you—or to the school." There was a longer pause this time. "Until we prove your innocence, both of you will take a little vacation."

Vacation? Sofia wondered. *Time off with pay, or with no salary?* They couldn't afford to miss many paychecks.

The science teacher slammed out first, storming past Sofia. She recognized the man with the shaggy hair and thick glasses from parent-teacher conferences. She thought he was even wearing the same gold cardigan. Jim followed right behind, his face so pale that it was almost the color of his bandage.

Sofia jumped up, but her weak legs buckled and she sat down hard. She stood again, avoiding Principal Piper's eyes, and hurried down the hall behind Jim, who didn't seem to remember she was there.

Yorkshire, England
July 1848

With her travel valise banging against her leg, Charlotte strode to the stairs to cross over the tracks. At the top, she grabbed a pole for support and caught her breath. *Curse those abominable stays!* Anne was a good bit behind her, but Charlotte stumbled ahead, across the footbridge, and down the steps on the other side.

A crowd had gathered around the Greens' first-class carriage. Mrs. Green continued to wail. "Help me! My daughter was murdered!" Her repeated screams died down until she moaned like a wounded animal.

The police constable—the one with huge canines that Charlotte had dubbed Mad Dog—was gentle despite his snarly appearance. He supported Mrs. Green with his large, scarred hands, lifting her bulk as if she were a featherweight. She fought and clawed at him as he led her away from the carriage. Two ladies stood helplessly by.

Suddenly, Mrs. Green's cries were cut off altogether, and she slumped into the police constable's arms. The ladies rushed forward to help support her other side as together they half-dragged Mrs. Green to the shade near the building and gently laid her on the ground.

For those moments, the carriage was unguarded. Charlotte raced to the open door. Like a tableau in a play, Mary remained in the same position in the corner of the carriage seat. Charlotte froze for a moment, shock mingled with sorrow for the death of one so young. However, as a curate's daughter, Charlotte was no stranger to death. She moved swiftly to check for a pulse. Fingers pressing firmly, she could detect nothing in wrist or neck. She wished she had a pocket mirror to hold beneath Mary's nose, in case she was breathing even the slightest bit. She truly looked peaceful.

So why had Mrs. Green screamed it was murder?

There were no obvious wounds, no blood or bruising or strangulation marks. Mary still wore her gloves, so if there had been any kind of struggle, there would be no signs like scraped knuckles or scratches from fighting someone off. Perhaps Mary had been much more ill than she'd thought.

Mary's lavender paisley shawl still lay over the back of the seat, but one thing had changed. Mary's drawstring, glass-beaded reticule was on the floor; her perfume, handkerchief, and fan had spilled out. The cinder glasses meant to protect her eyes from coal ashes were half hidden under Mary's skirt.

The clasp on her needlepoint valise was also undone. While it was impossible at a glance to tell if anything was missing, it appeared that someone had stirred the contents. Had it been searched?

If it weren't for the spilled reticule and the open valise, Charlotte would have assumed Mary's illness had taken an unexpected turn for the worse. But those things suggested Mary's death was a result of a robbery gone awry—unless Mrs. Green, in her panic, had knocked things about, trying to revive Mary.

Charlotte glanced over her shoulder. The police constable still knelt by Mrs. Green, who wasn't moving, and more people had gathered. She needed to move quickly. The carriage wouldn't be unguarded for more than another minute or two.

Poor Mary! She'd had so much to live for. Charlotte had a feeling that Mary would have found a way to be with her young man somehow. But now this.

Charlotte straightened to leave, but then a thought struck her. *The letters!* Mary would never want them read by a doctor who examined her. If the police constable saw them, they would be listed in official reports. Then newspaper reporters could find out about them. Charlotte knew from experience how cruel newspaper accounts could be. As a last act of kindness, Charlotte would take the packet of letters into safekeeping and mail them to Mrs. Green later. She would much rather mail them to the young man. If only she knew his identity.

Since her own reticule was small, she'd need to hide the letters in her carpetbag. She glanced over her shoulder again, then gently touched Mary. Sliding her fingers under the young woman's skirt band, she found the string she was looking for. She untied it from around Mary's waist and tugged, pulling out the strings. The slim packet of letters in the hidden pocket came with it. She jammed the letters in her carpetbag along with the trailing strings. Then, snapping the bag shut, she stepped backward out of the carriage.

It was not a moment too soon. The stationmaster, in his top hat and blue coat with polished buttons, had arrived to help the police constable disperse curious onlookers. One lady held smelling salts under Mrs. Green's nose, and she stirred, coughed, and came around. She immediately began shouting again from where she sat awkwardly on the ground.

"There's a murderer on this train! My poor Mary!"

The police officer wrapped his arm around Mrs. Green, gripped her arms with his massive hands, and lifted her to her feet as if the heavy woman weighed no more than a child.

She gripped the front of his coat. "I want Scotland Yard! Now!"

Charlotte sought Anne in the group that had gathered but didn't spot her. Scanning the area, Charlotte looked back toward the footbridge. Where had her sister gone?

Oh goodness. Anne was picking herself up off the platform. She was straightening her skirt and bonnet as Charlotte hurried to her side.

"What happened? Are you hurt?"

"I'm fine. I got in the way of a guard running to help Mrs. Green."

"And he knocked you down?"

"No. He was running by, and somehow the drawstring of my reticule got caught on his sleeve button. It jerked my wrist, and I stumbled and fell." She brushed at the dirt on the palm of her glove.

"Did he bother to stop and help?"

"Oh yes, the young man was very kind. He picked up what spilled when my reticule went flying." She pointed down the platform to a young guard striding toward the stationmaster's office. Charlotte's eyes narrowed as she studied the slender man's rolling gait. Was it her imagination, or had she seen that walk somewhere else recently?

The police constable and stationmaster were helping Mrs. Green to a long wooden bench near the waiting room. Charlotte wanted to help, but she had no idea what she could do for the poor, distraught woman. To lose a beloved daughter like that!

Charlotte edged through the cluster of passengers around Mrs. Green. "We've called your doctor," she heard the officer say. "He'll be here soon."

"I want an inspector or a superintendent!" Mrs. Green gripped the wooden arm of the bench and tried to throw herself forward. "Not some town constable."

The police constable gently forced her back onto the bench. "Wait, madam. The doctor will examine your daughter, but when I looked in your carriage, I didn't see any signs of foul play. Your daughter appears to have died peacefully in her sleep. I hope someday you can find some comfort in that."

Yes, Charlotte thought, *if it's true*. But she had an instinctive suspicion that the kind police constable was wrong.

"Let go!" Mrs. Green pushed his hand away. "I must get back to Mary!"

"She's being guarded," he said. "She's not alone, Mrs. Green. I'm Police Constable Griffiths, and you have my word on that. We'll move her off the train after the doctor attends to her."

Just then, Mrs. Green spotted Charlotte and Anne. "My Mary! She's dead!" she cried, tears streaming down her plump face. "She was tired when I went to find our manservant. He was late to pick us up. When I got back to the carriage, I couldn't wake her!"

The stationmaster, his fringe beard peppered with gray, brought Mrs. Green some tea. "I'm Stationmaster Woodford, ma'am." The short, wiry man held his head high and his back erect, as if trying to maximize his height.

Charlotte pulled him aside and asked, "Has Scotland Yard been called, as Mrs. Green requested?" Mary's rifled travel bag and reticule bothered her—a lot. She wanted to give her observances to someone official and higher up.

"No ma'am, not Scotland Yard. Any unexplained death occurring on the trains or in a station becomes a matter for the railway police. They will do the investigation." He pointed north. "Their nearest station house is a mile up the track that way. Their own railway constable has already been sent for." He breathed so deeply that his chest expanded. "I'll work directly with any inspector from Scotland Yard they might choose to call, but it's their choice."

Over the next hour, the stationmaster kept the unaffected trains and passengers moving in an orderly fashion. The family doctor, Dr. Thornton, arrived and examined Mary's body, then ordered her moved to the private back room in the stationmaster's office. He gave Mrs. Green a sedative and had her settled in the front room. Railway police told first-class passengers who'd been on the same London train as the Greens to remain for questioning.

Charlotte watched the controlled commotion from a slight distance, her sadness over Mary's death battling with suspicion. As she and Anne waited to be questioned, clouds built up from the north and moved in, dimming the sun as if the heavens, like Mrs. Green, were ready to weep.

4

Cabot Falls, Vermont
Present Day

The next day, Sofia just went through the motions at school. She wished fervently that she'd never promised to teach cake decorating and candy-making techniques. She showed up each morning wondering what rumors the teachers and students had heard, and it caused her to lose focus time and again.

And yet, as Jim told her, it was probably good that she had something else to focus on. Sofia got the distinct impression that he was relieved she wasn't at home dissecting the horrible turn of events all day long with him.

Jim had assured her that it was extremely unlikely that he'd lose his job. Even so, he didn't deserve to keep his job with a black cloud of suspicion hanging over his head. That would eat at him unbearably.

They downplayed the situation at home. Ten-year-old Matthew was impressed with his dad's stitches and thrilled that he had a few days off from work so they could bike ride and shoot baskets after school. On the other hand, Luke, at twelve, had come home Tuesday with a torn jacket. After school, a classmate with an older sibling at the high school had taunted him about his "criminal dad going to lockup," resulting in some pushing and shoving. This was so unlike their older son, who tended to be quiet like Jim. Sofia ached for him, knowing he was facing taunts about his dad.

She was talking with him about ignoring the nasty teasing when the phone rang. "Sofia? It's Julie. You okay?" Julie Butler, one of her friends in the weekly Pinot Painters group that met at Sofia's house, didn't sound like her usual bubbly self. "The twins saw Luke being picked on after school, and they heard some wild rumor about Jim losing his job."

"No, it's not quite that bad," Sofia said. She had debated telling her friends, wanting their emotional support, but she wasn't sure if Jim would mind. She was relieved to pour it out to Julie: the visit to the ER, the suspension, her worries about the kids. "Could you tell Marla for me?" Marla was Marla Dixon, the other painter in the group as well as the head librarian at the Cabot Falls Public Library.

"Will do," Julie said. "Call us if we can help. I mean it. We'll be praying."

"Thanks, and see you Saturday."

During supper, Sofia noticed that Vanessa and Wynter were unusually quiet. She stepped into their bedroom Tuesday night at bedtime and closed the door.

"You two all right?" Sofia asked.

"We're good," Vanessa said quickly.

Wynter nodded in agreement, which made Sofia suspicious immediately. Usually Wynter took the opposite view on anything Vanessa said, just out of principle.

"I've overheard a couple of hurtful statements at school," Sofia said. "Some speculation in the teachers' lounge when no one knew I was just outside."

Wynter stared at the floor. "If I hear anything like that, I'll knock the person flat."

Sofia gave them the eagle eye. "What's up?"

Vanessa sighed. "Mom, there will always be mean girls. So we decided to take a social media break for a while."

"You're getting bullied online?"

"Not really. Just a couple snide remarks." She glanced at Wynter. "It's better if we don't respond, and it's easy not to respond if we don't see them."

"You're very wise." Sofia hugged them both. "This whole thing should be cleared up soon." She hesitated. "You do know that your dad is innocent, right?"

"Mom!" Vanessa cried. "How can you even ask us that?"

"Just making sure." She had started to say something else when Jim called her name. She opened the girls' bedroom door. "What?"

"Rosa's on the phone," Jim yelled up the stairs.

"I'll take it in the bedroom," Sofia called back. "Good night, girls."

In the master bedroom, Sofia curled up in the wing chair by the window and picked up the extension. She hoped her sister hadn't heard about Jim's predicament somehow. She didn't feel like talking about it again.

"Sofia?" Rosa asked. "You have a minute?"

"Sure, but that's about all." Staring at the photo of her older sisters on her dresser, Sofia admitted they both looked striking and intelligent. PhD intelligent, both of them.

"Gina and I had lunch today. She asked me how the research was progressing with the eleventh square."

Sofia thought back to the weekend when she'd been working on the origin of the lavender paisley print. In the whirlwind of events, she hadn't given it a thought since.

"Um, let me think," Sofia said. "I researched which countries might have made the paisley-patterned silk fabric. So many countries made it."

"What about the diary? Have you translated anything from that yet?" Rosa was fluent in Italian, and Sofia had to admit that Nonna probably should have left the diary to her.

"My notes are downstairs, and I'm too tired to go get them."

Sofia thought back to why she'd had the wild idea about Charlotte Brontë. "I'm kind of excited about some of the Italian words that translate to 'Charlotte' and 'moor' and 'Jane.'"

"You've lost me," Rosa said.

"You know. The moors? Charlotte Brontë and *Jane Eyre*?"

Rosa laughed. "Sorry. I thought you were serious there for a minute."

Sofia fought down her hurt feelings. The week's events had left her emotionally raw. "I *am* serious. There were Italian words that translated into those English words."

"I think your infatuation with British authors is influencing your judgment."

"Why?"

"Because Nonna was Italian, like our mother. The quilt was found in Italy. So it stands to reason that the Italian words you found should be left in Italian with Italian meanings."

Sofia rubbed her throbbing temples. She'd done a fine job of tracking down the origins of the ten quilt squares so far. Couldn't her older sister give her the benefit of the doubt?

"Sofia?"

"Yes, I'm listening."

"Just think about it," Rosa said. "Instead of Charlotte, the name is probably Carlotta, like it says. Instead of Jane, it's Gianna. Don't you think you're making this too hard? Let the Italian names stay Italian."

Sofia made *umm*-ing noises.

"And you thought one Italian word was for 'moor'? I'm guessing the right translation is 'Mario' or some similar Italian name. Or even 'Mary.'"

Sofia blinked back tears, knowing that Rosa wasn't attacking her, even though it felt that way. She was exhausted and just wanted to get off the phone.

Fergus padded into the bedroom and gazed at her with bored interest, then slumped to the floor and rested his head on his paws with a drowsy sigh. Sofia wished she could join him.

She took a deep breath. Her sister, the New York City astrophysicist who worked at Cornell, always sounded so self-assured. "I can see your point, Rosa," Sofia said, reminding herself that Nonna had been Rosa's grandmother too. "You're probably right. I'll target my search in Italy with the Italian names instead."

Fergus looked up as if he were rolling his eyes at Sofia. She rolled hers back.

Yorkshire, England
July 1848

A quarter of an hour later, the railway constable arrived. Charlotte couldn't help noticing, with her writer's eye, how his frock coat and top hat were at variance with his large, round eyes that made him look as if he were in a state of constant surprise. He herded the remaining first-class passengers from the early morning train from London into the passenger waiting room.

"Sorry to detain you, folks," he said. "I'm Railway Constable Burton. I need your statements." His slight cockney accent marked him as a Londoner from the east side.

Charlotte took a quick inventory of the people in the room. Miss Oo-La-La was there, simpering at the men. Mr. Chin looked nervous, Muttonchops seemed annoyed at their delay, and Mr. Studious appeared curious, but nothing more.

Outgoing passengers passed through the waiting area, necks twisting in curiosity at the sight of the officer. Railway Constable Burton raised his voice over the commotion made by a family with five children who took seats amidst piled luggage and empty milk cans in the waiting room. "Normally, the railroad police spend the bulk of their time preventing accidents and sabotage on the rail line or theft of passenger luggage, goods, and coal." His round eyes gazed at each person in turn. "However, we also deal with crime once it's happened on the railroad."

Charlotte leaned forward, relieved. "So you're treating Miss Green's death as suspicious?"

In a slow circle, the railway constable swung his elaborately painted wooden truncheon topped with a silver crest of the railway company. "I need everyone's statements to make that determination, but yes, murder has been suggested."

"Suggested?" Anne whispered to Charlotte. "Mrs. Green was screaming 'Murder!' loud enough to be heard in London."

"If you'll follow me," the railway constable said, "we'll go down the street to the old St. John's Church. It will be quieter there to take your statements."

"How long will this take?" demanded Mr. Chin.

"The sooner we get to it, the sooner you can be on your way." Without waiting for other complaints, he led the way through the station to the street side. Wind whipped at Charlotte's bonnet strings, and she looked up. Clouds had piled up, darkening on the undersides to gunmetal gray. Thunder echoed to the west, and the wind brought damp-smelling air. She followed the small group to St. John's down the street.

Just before reaching the two-hundred-year-old church, Charlotte felt the first raindrops on her face. It became a fine drizzle by the time they all passed through the lych-gate into the little churchyard. Tombs, monuments, and stone crosses were clustered together at odd angles, surrounded by uncut grass and brambles. The old church showed clear signs of ruin.

They left the morning drizzle and entered the chill interior of the building. The first-class passengers gathered at the back of the church. Wooden pews made of black oak ran down either side, but Charlotte saw no worshipers there other than a woman in black kneeling in the front pew. A vicar with long, wavy, graying hair sat beside her but swung around as they entered. He stood to approach them, but the railway constable gave a decided shake of his head, and the puzzled-looking vicar rejoined the woman.

"I'll make this as short as possible so you can get on your way." The officer stood against a pillar along the side of the nave. "Ladies first." He nodded at the attractive Miss Oo-La-La and led her away from the group.

She straightened, patted her blond hair, and shivered dramatically. "It's cold in here!" she said, rubbing her bare arms.

Charlotte knew how voices carried in echoing, cavernous churches, and she listened to her interview while pretending to study the small stained glass windows. With little effort, she could hear the railway constable's questions. Name? It turned out that Miss Oo-La-La was Celia May. What was her business in London? She had been visiting her aunt and uncle in Lancaster Street. Charlotte studied her out of the corner of her eye.

"I was orphaned as a child, but they raised me." Her eyes glistened, and she dropped her gaze. "Now I'm on my own. I'm on my way home to Liverpool." Then Miss May said she'd joined the Greens' carriage at the Sheffield station, but they hadn't spoken. "The young woman had seemed unwell," she said. "When I tried to talk to her, her fierce mama *glared* at me, so I backed off." She waved her slender fingers and fluttered her eyelashes.

The railway constable wrote in his notebook, apparently

impervious to her charms. Charlotte suspected that Celia May rarely got that kind of response. He tore a sheet from his notepad and handed it to her with a pencil. "Write down your current address, in case we need to contact you later. Then that will be all."

After she finished, he motioned for Anne to join him next, but Muttonchops stepped forward. "Excuse me, but I'll miss my connection if I'm not interviewed next."

"Ladies first," Railway Constable Burton said calmly.

"I don't mind waiting," Anne said.

Charlotte leaned over and whispered, "Let's go last if we can." Anne raised an eyebrow in question. "He's asking about our reasons for being in London. I don't want everyone in this room to know. There's no privacy here."

"You're right."

Charlotte let the railway constable know that they would buy tickets for a later train to Keighley. Even though Celia May had been interviewed, she didn't leave. It might have been because of the rain running down the windows, but Charlotte doubted it. She'd already mentioned more than once that she was "traveling alone." While Mr. Studious simply gave her a courteous nod before turning away—and Charlotte admired him for it—Mr. Chin eagerly kept her company, comparing notes on their favorite restaurants and theaters in London.

"Have you seen Jenny Lind as Elvira in *I Puritani*?" Mr. Chin asked. "I saw her perform last night at the Garden."

Charlotte nudged her sister. "Did you hear that? He's lying. The play at the theater last night was *The Barber of Seville*."

"But how do we know that that was the only play at Covent Garden last night? London has *dozens* of theaters."

Charlotte shrugged, then concentrated on the questions being asked next. Muttonchops's name turned out to be Edward Smithwick; he was a well-to-do fire and life insurance agent. His voice boomed. "I represent the Albion Fire and Life Assurance Company, of 42 New Bridge Street, based in London but with offices in North America, Australia, Germany, and Denmark."

"And you were on the train today because . . . ?" the railway constable asked, scribbling quickly.

"I travel to settle claims for big businesses." His whiskers fluttered as he rocked back and forth on the balls of his feet. "I thoroughly investigate claims before paying out a single pence or pound."

Charlotte tilted her head slightly. Something in Muttonchops's story didn't ring true. Albion Fire and Life was a gigantic company. A claims agent for big businesses would surely make a sizable income, but that didn't match his frayed coat cuffs or the worn heels of his boots.

"Did you speak to the victim today?" the railway constable asked.

"No, I wasn't in her carriage," Mr. Smithwick said, sounding confused. "I had no idea who the Greens were."

Charlotte noted Anne's frown. "What is it?"

Anne pulled Charlotte away from the others. "I could be wrong—I probably am—but . . ."

"But what?"

"When you and Mary were talking on the bench at Sheffield Station, Mrs. Green was still in her carriage. Our doors were open, and Mr. Smithwick walked by and stopped at their carriage. He talked to someone—I couldn't see who, but it certainly sounded like Mrs. Green."

"Could you hear what he said?"

"He recognized her from some London event she'd attended with her husband. I remember Mrs. Green telling him that her husband was in France at a conference."

Charlotte nodded. "She was intent on impressing us with that information too."

Mr. Studious joined them and made a small bow. The candle flames from the wall sconce reflected in his oval eyeglasses. "Are you quite sure you don't mind if I go before you?"

Charlotte shook her head. "We don't mind at all, Mr. . . . ?"

"Hopkins, George Hopkins." He straightened his tie and excused himself to join the railway constable.

Charlotte sat in the back pew and could hear even more easily now that the rain had stopped. She heard that Mr. Hopkins was a schoolmaster on holiday who'd been visiting London. That explained the book satchel and more casual attire, Charlotte thought. She had great respect for teachers and thought it was the hardest job she had ever undertaken.

"And your school is where?" the officer asked.

"Doncaster School for the Deaf," he said. "I'm on my way back there after checking with some London museums, to ask which ones might accommodate my students."

"Must be a challenging line of work," the railway constable said.

"Yes, but rewarding."

Charlotte's respect for him grew even more. Her best friend had a nephew who was deaf. Doncaster was only thirty minutes southeast from Leeds by train, but Charlotte believed the nephew was southwest, at the Manchester School for the Deaf.

Railway Constable Burton swung his truncheon back and forth. "Is there anything useful you can teach deaf students so they can operate in the real world?"

"Oh yes, they learn trades. Many of our boys are learning to make shoes."

"So they go on to lead normal lives?"

"Most find employment in a trade we train them for," Mr. Hopkins said. "You won't find our Doncaster lads begging in the streets."

Charlotte smiled at Anne. So far, the schoolmaster was the

most impressive. A minute later, Mr. Smithwick and Mr. Hopkins left the church together, with Celia May between them because "I need to lean on a strong man's arm."

Mr. Chin watched them leave, looking angry at being excluded. "How long is this going to take?" he muttered. He pulled out his pocket watch, read the time, and snapped it shut. How scratched and uncared for his watch looked, Charlotte thought, compared to her father's treasured timepiece. It was odd that a man who frequented expensive London restaurants and entertainment would carry such a scratched watch.

The constable summoned Mr. Chin.

"Name?" the officer asked.

"James Thomas."

"And Mr. Thomas, what was your business in London?" the constable asked.

"Visiting physicians and hospitals. I'm a traveling salesman for a medical equipment company, Simon & Engels."

"And you live where?"

"On Canal Road in Keighley." His chin jutted out even farther. "I'm on my way home."

Charlotte perked up at that. Canal Road? She wasn't sure there were homes on Canal Road. Or was she remembering wrong? Since she and Anne had to travel north to Keighley too, she'd take time to check it out before they started walking the last few miles to Haworth.

The moment that Railway Constable Burton was finished, James Thomas hurried from the church, his heels clicking on the stone floor. "And now, ladies . . . ," the officer said.

But before he could ask them any questions, Police Constable Griffiths rushed into the church, tracking rainwater across the flagstones. He waved one large, badly scarred hand. "Sir, the cause of death has been decided."

Charlotte's back was rigid as she braced for the dreaded news.

5

Cabot Falls, Vermont
Present Day

Thursday after school, Sofia was grateful to pick up the boys and Wynter and head home. Vanessa had arranged a ride after play rehearsal, so Sofia was looking forward to putting her feet up for a while. Her cake decorating classes had gone well, but she was so bone weary. She'd be relieved when her teaching commitment was over.

She pulled into the garage, and the boys piled out of the car. She heard Matthew call out, "Hi, Mrs. Cooper!"

Sofia closed her eyes and froze behind the wheel. *Please, not today*, she thought. She liked Pat Cooper—a lot, actually—but today she just wanted to collapse and veg out.

Taking a deep breath, Sofia fixed a smile on her face and stepped out of the Suburban. "Pat, hi, how are you? Good class today?"

The octogenarian, spry way beyond her years, was already in their driveway. In her pink leg warmers and tights, she'd obviously just returned from her exercise class.

"I'm going to relax with a cup of coffee," Sofia said. "Join me?"

"Sure, if you don't mind," Pat said. "I noticed this week that Jim didn't go to work. Is he all right?"

Sofia waited until all the kids had gone in the house, then summarized the break-in and their trip to the ER Sunday night. "Nothing was vandalized in Jim's math room, and the locked desk wasn't tampered with. Jim may have interrupted someone looking for money."

Pat followed her inside. "What else is bothering you?"

Sofia bit her lower lip and debated how much to tell her. Pat had been her teacher when Sofia was in high school, and she'd proved herself to be a good friend and good neighbor since then. So after making coffee, they stood at the living room window and watched the children with Jim in the backyard. Sofia summarized the situation at school.

"I can help, you know," Pat said. "I know about perps."

Sofia smiled. Pat was part of their neighborhood COP program, a Citizens on Patrol watch group that was the eyes and ears for the police force in their community. Mostly, Sofia thought, it gave Pat a reason to call her old English student, Officer Quimby, whenever she observed something suspicious. That's actually why Pat was taking an exercise class. Worried that she might not be able to handle a perp if she cornered one, she enrolled in a class at the gym for strength training. The class, run by a young trainer named Destiny, was called Change Your Destiny with Destiny.

They finished their coffee and put the cups in the sink. "What's this?" Pat asked.

Sofia glanced at the pile of kids' papers from their backpacks dumped on the counter. "It's a brochure advertising our high school's grandparent tutoring program." She explained how Mr. Jeffries had been helping Wynter.

Pat read part of it aloud. "SHiPS—Special Helpers in Public Schools. A grandparent can help in many ways: tutoring individuals in music, math, carpentry, cooking, science, homework assistance, helping in the classroom or library, helping with office assistance or the publishing center." Pat's eyes gleamed below her striped sweatband. "I know. I'll volunteer at the school as part of the program. It will give me a reason to be in the school so I can help you investigate."

"That's not necessary. Anyway, you don't have a grandchild at the high school."

"No problem. You can vouch for me. Say that I'm your children's unofficial grandparent."

"Are you sure you want to do that?"

"I still remember my way around the school," Pat assured her. "I'll be the perfect spy. No one notices old people. You become invisible at my age. I'll be able to get into places you can't."

"I know but . . ." Sofia touched her friend's arm. "You're very strong for your age, but that intruder knocked Jim and me down."

"You were taken by surprise," Pat said. "I'll keep my eyes open. Don't worry."

Too exhausted to argue, Sofia nodded and thanked her former teacher. "Just be careful, Pat. We have no idea who's behind the grade fixing, but someone's already attacked Jim. They won't be afraid of me—or you."

Yorkshire, England
July 1848

Charlotte held her breath as they all waited for the dripping Police Constable Griffiths to give them the news.

"Yes?" the railway officer prompted.

"The family doctor has attributed Mary Green's death to a disease she had been suffering from for some time."

"That's ridiculous!" Charlotte cried, sputtering. "You don't die from nervous prostration."

Police Constable Griffiths referred to his notes. "The family doctor didn't agree with the London specialist on that diagnosis. He believed Miss Green had something more serious." He closed his notebook. "Dr. Thornton feels Miss Green either took an overdose of her prescription on purpose or took too much by accident for the pain."

Railway Constable Burton nodded slowly. "That's certainly possible."

"No it isn't!" Charlotte cried.

"Charlotte, what's wrong with you?" Anne hissed. "We don't know anything about it."

Charlotte bit back the words on her tongue. She'd talked to Mary Green. She was a girl in love, eager to see her young man again, determined that love was going to conquer all. She didn't take an overdose on purpose. But then . . . Charlotte realized she had no idea if Mary could have overdosed accidentally because of the pain. The family doctor could be right.

Railway Constable Burton nodded his thanks to the watching vicar, then ushered them toward the door leading to the graveyard. Outside, Police Constable Griffiths blocked the path. "Excuse me, but that wasn't all, sir. Mrs. Green won't go home with the servant who came for her. She keeps screaming 'murder' to anyone who will listen, and it's creating a ruckus at the train station. She says it can't be suicide either. She also doesn't believe it to be an accidental overdose."

The railway constable slapped his leg with his truncheon. "Does she say why not?"

"Yes. The daughter had taken the same prescription for months. She wouldn't suddenly make that kind of mistake. So, in her mind, it must be murder."

Charlotte caught Anne's eye and gave a slight shake of her head. She needed to confide in her sister before either of them talked to the railway constable. She cleared her throat.

"Excuse me," she said, "but could my sister and I walk back to the station for some, um, refreshment?" She wanted the privacy of the lavatory, but under no circumstances could she ask him for permission to use the facilities.

"We'll walk back with you, and I'll take your statements there." The railway constable studied Charlotte, his wide eyes now narrowed. "Am I right in assuming you knew the deceased?"

"Not especially," Charlotte said, "but I talked to her at Sheffield for a few minutes." *And I checked the crime scene. And I took something important from Mary's body.* No, she couldn't say that. Even Anne would be aghast when Charlotte told her.

On the walk back to the station, Charlotte waded absently through puddles. What about those letters now? Were they really simple love letters from a young but unsuitable man? Or was there more to it that Mary hadn't admitted? Could they have been written by someone in the public eye instead, someone who had important reasons for their relationship to be kept quiet? *Did this man keep Mary quiet permanently?*

Charlotte tripped at that thought, and Anne caught her arm. Charlotte barely noticed.

Could that be why Mary's reticule and valise showed evidence of a hasty search? Had someone tried to retrieve the letters and silence Mary at the same time?

Charlotte knew she was just speculating. She could no longer postpone reading the letters on the train ride home. She had to read them now.

But first, she had to find some privacy.

When they arrived at the station, Railway Constable Burton bowed to the ladies. "Will you come to the stationmaster's office in ten minutes? I'll be outside."

Charlotte would have agreed to anything to escape his prying eyes. She nodded, then hurried off arm in arm with Anne. In hushed tones, she explained what she'd taken from Mary and where she had the letters.

"What? You did—you did . . ." Anne stammered, but in the end, words failed her.

"I know, I know. I'll explain later." Inside the lavatory, Charlotte entered a stall and dug in her travel bag for Mary's secret pocket of letters.

The four letters were tied together with a pink satin ribbon. Squelching her guilt about reading another person's mail, she selected one. The two sheets of paper inside were thin, and words filled every available space. She read the cramped writing as quickly as possible. She couldn't stay in the stall forever, despite Anne chatting to the attendant to divert her attention.

Charlotte's eyes skimmed down the page. ". . . loved seeing you at the music competition . . . your sweet voice . . . meet me alone when we next go to the seaside . . . I dream of you . . ." There was more in the same vein, confirming what Mary had told her. She skipped to the second page at the bottom for the signature.

But there was none.

Just the initials N.S.

Outside the stall, either Anne or the attendant cleared her throat. Charlotte knew they had to go meet the railway constable. She'd have to read the other letters later. She stuffed the letters back into Mary's secret pocket.

Charlotte lifted her skirt and top petticoat. Holding the hem of her skirt between her teeth, she laid Mary's pocket of letters flat against her stomach, then tied the heavy threads behind her like apron strings. The flat pocket would never show under the skirt and petticoat.

Hidden, just as Mary had counted on herself.

Had someone wanted those letters enough to kill for them? Were they that valuable? Then a sudden thought struck her. *Could the killer have wanted them in order to blackmail Mary's father, the banker?* He would be the one with the money to pay—and he'd want to protect his daughter's reputation if N.S. proved to be an unsavory character.

Charlotte tipped the attendant on her way out and explained outside to Anne about what she'd read and what she speculated it might mean.

"I don't understand," Anne said. "If this was a secret relationship, how would a thief have even known about it or known she had the letters?"

"First, the thief might have been Mary's young man himself. If it was someone else, Mary and her young man must have told someone. Or they were seen together in London where they met. She said they met in public places." Charlotte tried to remember more details. "She also mentioned a photo of them together, maybe something he could use for blackmail."

"Was there a photo in the letters?"

"I don't know. I only had time to open one envelope." She stopped talking and motioned up ahead where Railroad Constable Burton was waiting.

As they passed the waiting room, a man rushed out onto the platform and nearly plowed into them. "Oh, excuse me," he said, tipping his hat. It was Mr. Chin, James Thomas from Keighley, seller of medical equipment.

"Eager to get home?" Charlotte asked.

"What?" He scanned the crowd up and down the tracks. "Uh, no, I was actually looking for Miss Celia May. She hasn't left already, has she?"

"I have no idea."

A shout near the first-class carriage diverted Charlotte's attention. A short, thin guard down the platform was wrestling a large suitcase to hand up to the guard on top of the carriage.

He tried to lift it, but it fell back to the platform. He pushed his loose hat down on his head and tried again. When the second attempt failed, a porter stepped up, grabbed the case, and tossed it up with apparent ease. *How embarrassing for that poor guard,* Charlotte thought.

When she turned back, James Thomas had disappeared.

At the stationmaster's office, the railway constable waited outside. Loud voices echoed from within. Mrs. Green's voice was as robust as ever, despite the obvious grief of her words.

"Dr. Thornton, she wouldn't kill herself!" Mrs. Green cried.

"I'm not saying she did," a calmer voice replied. "I know you're distraught. Of course you would be. I'm sure the overdose was accidental."

"No, she was murdered! Did that *constable* get someone yet to take over?" she demanded, hysteria raising her voice half an octave. "Mary's father has money, and money talks. I want an inspector! And if I don't get one immediately, they will hear about it! I'll go straight to the deputy assistant commissioner if I have to!"

The railway constable motioned for the Brontë sisters to move away from the door. "Let's talk over there," he said. They moved about twenty feet along the platform.

Anne gulped visibly. "Is poor Mrs. Green in that office with, um, her daughter?"

"Yes, but Mary's body is still in the back room where the doctor examined her. They are waiting for the body to be moved home." He cleared his throat. "As you may have gathered, Mrs. Green has demanded Scotland Yard take over the investigation into her daughter's death. That won't happen." He cleared his throat. "Instead, Railway Inspector Tipp from London will arrive as soon as possible, but I don't know how much good it will do. Railway inspectors deal with crime on the rail line, not accidental death or suicide."

Anne frowned. "So we have to wait till he arrives and give our statements to him?"

"No, he telegraphed, and I am to take the remaining statements from witnesses. He will contact you if he needs you further. Despite Mrs. Green's protests, this is a sad incident, but nothing more."

Charlotte didn't agree, but could she make him see her point without revealing Mary's personal life and adding to her mother's already intense grief?

"But what if Mrs. Green is right?" Charlotte said. "You should call in local Leeds constables and all the railway police up and down the line before a killer gets away."

"I think you have an unrealistic idea of our strength," he said. "The local Leeds station has a staff of only twenty-one officers for the whole city around the clock. As for the railway police, the building of railroad lines has outstripped our ability to protect it. In the last four years alone, some four thousand miles of new railway lines have opened."

"I didn't know," Charlotte admitted. "But even so, if the doctor is wrong, you should have police all over, combing the crime scene area."

Railway Constable Burton eyed Charlotte with new interest. "Crime scene? Why did you call it that?" He tilted his head. "Miss Brontë, what do you know?"

6

Cabot Falls, Vermont
Present Day

Friday after supper, Sofia drove back to the high school to pick up Vanessa. Their spring play would be performed in just three weeks, and the rehearsals were long. Although Vanessa was assigned to the stage backdrops and other painting, she had to work as late as the actors.

Sofia pulled into the parking lot at the same time as Mr. Jeffries. She waved when she got out of the Suburban. His grandson, Adam, also was involved in theater. Adam arranged the lighting, plus he videotaped the play practices so they could watch them the next day and make improvements.

Sofia fell into step beside Mr. Jeffries, but she immediately felt the strain between them, a strain that had never been there before. As they talked about the play, she suspected that they were both remembering the explosive scene in the principal's office on Monday.

Reaching the auditorium, Mr. Jeffries turned to Sofia and cleared his throat. "I just wanted to say . . ." He stopped, looking acutely uncomfortable. "I mean, I don't want to pretend I don't know . . ." He stopped again and gave Sofia a small smile. "I just wanted to say how sorry I am about what is happening with the teachers. I have no doubt that your husband is innocent of any wrongdoing."

Tears sprang to Sofia's eyes, and it surprised her. Most of the teachers and all of the students had tiptoed around the subject all week, not mentioning Jim's suspension and cutting conversations short when Sofia came into view. It was a relief and a kindness to have someone from the school mention it.

Sofia gripped Mr. Jeffries's arm briefly. "Your words mean a lot to me. Thank you."

He nodded, then held open the door to the auditorium for her to enter.

They stood together at the back until the director finished critiquing the last segment the students had rehearsed. The play, *Sixteen in 10 Minutes or Less*, was ten short mini plays on the angst of being sixteen. Because there were so many segments, it required a tremendous amount of backdrop changes, props, and scenery painting.

When the faculty director dismissed them, Vanessa and Adam strolled up the aisle together.

"Say, Mrs. Parker," Adam said, pulling a notepad from his back pocket, "I don't have you down for a video of the play yet. How many copies do you want to preorder?"

Vanessa poked him in the ribs. "You can't sell copies," she said, rolling her eyes.

Sofia laughed. "Wish you could though."

"Me too," Adam said. "I videotape the play using three different cameras in three locations. The computer teacher volunteered to cut and splice it all, showing the play from all the best angles, but the director said it's a no-go. Some copyright issue or something."

"Well, see you later, Adam." Vanessa headed out the door. "What's for supper, Mom?"

Sofia smiled, grateful that for the kids, anyway, life was going forward without much change. The kids knew Jim had contacted a lawyer and assumed the misunderstanding at school would get straightened out soon.

Sofia put an arm around Vanessa as they crossed the parking lot. As long as possible, she planned to let the children believe that all would be well.

Yorkshire, England
July 1848

Charlotte squirmed inwardly under Railway Constable Burton's intense scrutiny.

"I repeat," he said, "what makes you think we have a crime scene?"

"Instinct," Charlotte finally said.

The railway constable kept a straight face, but it looked like a challenge. "Would that be women's intuition?"

Charlotte felt her temper flare, and she angled her face so her bonnet hid her expression. *What a patronizing comment.* She knew without benefit of a mirror that her eyes were "snapping," as Papa described it.

She finally raised her gaze to meet his. "I didn't mean to tell you how to do your job."

The railway constable pulled out his notebook and pencil. "Let me get your statements. Then you're free to go."

Charlotte took the lead. "I'm Charlotte Brontë, and we live at the Haworth parsonage with our father, Patrick Brontë, the curate. We're on our way home now." She stopped with finality, hoping she conveyed the message that that was all she had to say.

He made a note. "And what was your business in London, Miss Brontë?"

"Last night, we attended the opera at Covent Garden."

The railway constable's pencil paused. Charlotte guessed what he was thinking, considering how plainly they were dressed and knowing they lived in a parsonage. Neither she nor Anne looked anything like the fancy ladies they'd seen at the theater the night before.

"You went to London to see an opera," he repeated. "Is that the only reason you were in London?"

Charlotte gripped her travel bag to stop her hand from shaking. She had been forced to tell their publisher their true identities so the speculation in the press could be squelched. But she had no intention of going public about their writing activities. As their father often reminded them, secrecy was paramount. Being in publishing was no occupation for ladies.

Railway Constable Burton shuffled his feet a bit, then rephrased his question. "Miss Brontë, in light of the fact that you seem convinced we have a crime on our hands, I must request that you answer my question. What other business required you to be on this particular train at this particular time?"

Charlotte stood her ground. He couldn't make her talk, and she wasn't breaking any laws by being quiet, as far as she knew.

The silence dragged on. Then the railway constable flipped to a new page. "And your name is?" he asked, turning toward her sister.

"Anne," she squeaked. Clearing her throat, she repeated, "Anne. Anne Brontë. Also of Haworth." Anne shot Charlotte a look of pure panic.

"Perhaps *you* can tell me why you were in London, other than seeing the opera." His voice was smooth, even friendly, Charlotte thought, and she bet his wide eyes were supposed to invite confidence. *Don't tell, Anne*, she hoped her expression said loud and clear.

People swirled around them, and a goods train rushed by at high speed, clattering down the center rail between the platforms.

"There will probably be no need for me to tell anyone your reason for being in London," Railway Constable Burton said after the noise had subsided. "On the other hand, in order to eliminate you from our inquiries, you must tell me." He waited. Nothing. "Ladies, trust me. You don't want me to hold you until Inspector Tipp arrives and interviews you himself. He might not arrest you, but he can delay your journey home as long as he needs to."

Charlotte studied Anne's face. It was drained of color, and she seemed to shrink even smaller. Charlotte had promised Anne that if she came to London to prove who they were, no one but their publishers would have to know. And she'd meant it. If their occupation became public, there would be ridicule and scorn, not just for themselves, but also aimed at their father.

Finally, Charlotte spoke, if for no other reason than to avoid detainment. "You have never heard of *Jane Eyre*, but—"

"The book?" the officer asked.

Charlotte blinked in surprise. "Yes, the book. Have you read it?"

"No, but my wife and sister have. They couldn't stop talking about it."

Anne looked slightly less frightened, and Charlotte breathed a bit easier.

"We were in London yesterday to see our publisher. I wrote *Jane Eyre*. My sister wrote *The Tenant of Wildfell Hall*."

The railway constable stopped taking notes. "You wrote *Jane Eyre*?" He brushed a hand over his mouth. "I happen to know that that book was written by Currer Bell. My sister went on and on about him, wondering how he could understand a woman's feelings so well . . ."

At Anne's laugh, his voice trailed off in doubt. "It's because Currer Bell is Charlotte," she said.

Charlotte nodded. "I knew how a teacher and governess would feel because I've been a teacher, at Cowan Bridge School, and I've been a governess, just like Jane." Glancing around, she lowered her voice. "I am Currer Bell. My sister, Anne, is Acton Bell. We have a third sister at home, Emily, who is Ellis Bell. She wrote *Wuthering Heights*."

Railway Constable Burton took notes on this, but he didn't look convinced. "Can you offer any proof that you are the, uh, authoresses you claim to be?"

Good grief, Charlotte thought. She'd broken her word to her sister and revealed their true identities, and now he wanted proof.

"What is the problem?" she demanded. "Do you think that a demented woman who believes she is an author boarded the train in order to create her own crime scene?"

"You have to admit, ma'am, that if you wrote that book, you're clever at making things up."

"It's called being creative, not 'making things up,'" Charlotte snapped.

Anne reached out and tentatively tugged on Charlotte's sleeve. "Did you keep the correspondence with our publisher?" she whispered.

"I did!" Charlotte knelt down and opened her travel bag. Tucked down the side was the correspondence between their publisher in London and the Bell brothers in Haworth. She'd used that correspondence to prove to the publisher that they were the authors. She pulled the letters out and stood. "Here." She thrust them under Railway Constable Burton's nose.

While he read through both letters with official letterhead, Charlotte gazed about her. Her eye was caught when she spotted James Thomas, chin jutting ahead of him as he strolled down the platform with a newspaper folded under his arm. He glanced around him as if he were lost. Then his homely face lit up when he turned toward the end of the short train.

Charlotte spotted Miss Celia Oo-La-La mincing down the platform, heading their way. She was fanning herself against the heat that rose up from the platform, now that the rain had stopped. With her other hand, she patted her intricately coiffed blond hair. James Thomas made a beeline for her.

Railway Constable Burton cleared his throat. "I apologize for not believing you at first."

Anne smiled. "Don't worry. Our own publisher required proof before he believed us." She paused. "Are we free to go home then?"

Before he could answer, the door to the stationmaster's office flew open. Mrs. Green charged out, her face red and blotchy, her wild eyes riveted on the Brontë sisters.

"Constable, stop those thieves!"

7

Cabot Falls, Vermont
Present Day

On Saturday morning, Sofia rolled out of bed early, but Jim's side of the bed was already cold. He was waking up earlier and earlier these days, she'd noticed.

Before his suspension, Sofia had made arrangements with her Pinot Painter friends to get together on Saturdays instead of Wednesday afternoons. So Marla and Julie would be arriving at nine thirty that morning.

"At least I've got leftovers to serve," she muttered, glad she'd brought home her demonstration cakes with buttercream flower decorations. Next week, she'd have candy samples for her Pinot Painter friends.

Sofia just hoped that Luke and Matthew hadn't foraged for snacks already that morning. Since she'd been catering, Sofia noticed that her bakery leftovers seemed to disappear fast on the weekends.

Marla and Julie wouldn't mind having her family underfoot this morning. It wouldn't be their usual, esoteric, "glass of wine, paint, and talk about art" afternoon. More of a "cake and milk and kids" morning instead.

However, Jim took the boys with him to look at a new lawn mower, so that cut the traffic through the house by half and saved what was left of her mini cakes. Sofia suspected Jim also was avoiding any well-meaning questions from her friends.

By ten o'clock, Marla and Julie were there, easels set up in the four-season room, with Vanessa looking over their shoulders as they painted.

"So how's the play coming?" Marla asked, pushing wavy blond hair out of the way. "Tim says your backdrops are the best part of the show."

Vanessa took a bow. "Tim is really quite good himself," she said, referring to Marla's fifteen-year-old son. "I didn't know he could sing like that. Why isn't he in chorus?"

Marla stretched, so lean and athletic that she could pass for a teenager. "You know boys. It would interfere with baseball practice."

"Jocks." Vanessa rolled her eyes. "See ya later." She went upstairs, and Wynter followed.

The trio painted in silence for ten minutes, then Sofia put down her brush. "I'll set out the food for whenever you're hungry."

When she returned, Sofia got the impression that she'd interrupted a conversation. Maybe she was being paranoid after the number of times sudden silences had happened to her at the school.

"Have you made any headway on the eleventh quilt block yet?" Marla asked. As head librarian at the Cabot Falls Public Library, she had been an immense help to Sofia at different times. She had access to official websites at the library, especially those on genealogy, that Sofia didn't have without paying a hefty subscription price.

"I thought I was onto something rather exciting," Sofia admitted. She told them about her wild idea that somehow Charlotte Brontë was involved in the making of her quilt square. "But Rosa made some good points, and she's convinced that the paisley print originated in Italy and that the words I translated as 'Jane' and 'moors' and 'Charlotte' are probably just Italian words: 'Gia,' '*moro*,' 'Carlotta.'"

Julie wiggled her fingers at Sofia, her elegantly polished nails the pastel colors of Easter eggs. "Well, we know how you love those English authors," she teased, her green eyes dancing.

"True," Sofia admitted.

Marla finished her small cake, licking every bit of buttercream frosting off her fingers. "Think about this though. Nonna gave *you* the quilt to decipher. She felt *you* were the sister to dig out the true meanings behind each block. Maybe your grandmother knew that, because of your wider interests, you'd be willing to look beyond the borders of Italy for your answers." She set her cake plate on an end table. "Some of the other quilt blocks were related to famous people in other countries, including America."

Julie agreed. "Your gut instinct is just as likely to be right as Rosa's."

Sofia smiled. She loved her friends. "Well, the little I've done on the computer trying it Rosa's way hasn't gotten me anywhere." She began picking up their plates and napkins. "And I reread Nonna's letter to me, the one that came with the diary. She *did* think I was the best one to track down the history of the quilt."

"Mwa-ha-ha," Julie said in her best, most evil tone. "The mystery of the history."

Sofia threw a crumpled paper napkin at her. How good it felt to laugh again.

Yorkshire, England
July 1848

Dr. Thornton ran out after Mrs. Green and tried to pull her

back into the stationmaster's office, but Mrs. Green broke free of his grasp and ran into a crowd of passengers.

"My daughter was murdered on that train. And her body was robbed!"

Railway Constable Burton raced forward and, along with Dr. Thornton, bodily turned her around. But nothing would stop her repeated screams.

Mary's body was robbed? Charlotte glanced at her sister and recognized her own fears reflected in Anne's eyes. Mrs. Green must have known about the letters after all and just discovered that they were missing.

After helping the distraught mother back into the office, the railway constable returned. He strode to the Brontë sisters. "Stay here," he said brusquely and hurried off to where Celia May was buying food from a vendor. He spoke to her briefly, and it was clear to Charlotte that Miss May was arguing with him. When she returned with the railway constable, everything about her, from her pouting lips to her dragging feet, showed her reluctance to cooperate.

"What's going on?" Charlotte asked.

The officer's formerly relaxed demeanor had turned grim. "Dr. Thornton gave Isobel Green her daughter's personal effects. Mrs. Green claims that many things are missing: a bracelet watch, an ornamental mirror and brush, and other valuables."

Celia tapped the point of her parasol on the platform. "I'm sure that's very sad, but what does that have to do with me?"

Charlotte nearly rolled her eyes. Could she really be that dense? "Mrs. Green thinks one of us stole her daughter's belongings."

"Well, *I* didn't!" Celia snapped.

Railway Constable Burton stretched his arms wide, as if trying to herd the ladies forward. "If you ladies would step this way, we can settle the question right now."

Anne frowned at Charlotte. Were they being detained after all? They moved forward quietly. Charlotte stiffened as they passed into the office, but she soon realized that the officer had been correct: Mary's body wasn't in the front part of the office.

It was crowded, but Mrs. Green had finally stopped shouting. Charlotte thought she had never seen anyone so angry and so grief-stricken at the same time.

Railway Constable Burton cleared his throat. "You ladies were asked in here because you were the only ladies in the first-class carriages early this morning. You, Miss May, talked with the deceased and rode in her carriage. The Misses Brontë rode in the carriage right behind Mary, and they had occasion to get acquainted between trains."

"Is that a crime?" Miss May demanded.

"No, but stealing from my Mary is!" Mrs. Green cried.

"We can settle this quickly," the railway constable said. "Please open your bags for me. While you watch, I will search for the missing items. If all is well, you'll be free to go."

Celia May stood rigidly and crossed her arms tight across her chest. "If you touch my things, there will be repercussions."

Charlotte was indignant as well. "You have no search warrant!"

"I can go to the magistrate and get one," he said agreeably, "but it will postpone your departure."

"I want to go home," Anne pleaded.

Fuming, Charlotte held her head high and opened her bag wide. "I have nothing to hide." Of course, that wasn't quite true. She didn't have any of Mary's jewelry, but the packet of letters was nestled underneath her top petticoat. Charlotte was grateful that the constable wasn't checking hidden pockets.

If Anne hadn't begged her to go home—and if Charlotte weren't afraid of the horrible publicity that would ensue if she complained to the constable's superintendent—she would have refused to have her belongings searched. She glanced over at Mrs. Green, who had collapsed on a chair not designed to hold a woman her size, and relented. Of course she wanted her daughter's things back. While Charlotte knew that neither she nor Anne had taken them, she was not as sure about Celia May.

Railway Constable Burton motioned for the doctor to escort Mrs. Green outside, and Charlotte was grateful. The woman's grief was so raw. While her outbursts were understandable, they were still unnerving.

Searching Celia's belongings took only a minute, and then she left in a huff. Charlotte was next. The constable took five minutes but found none of the missing items in her hand luggage or reticule. When the constable tightened the drawstring on Charlotte's purse and tossed it back to her, Charlotte gasped. She had a sudden image of seeing something tossed from the train near a stone bridge before coming into Leeds.

"I remember something!" she cried. "I bet your thief threw the stolen items off the train in a cloth bag or something. Please send someone to search near the stone bridge just outside of Leeds. Even if the bag has already been collected, you might see the footprints of whoever picked it up."

"I'll look into it." While the railway constable made a note, Charlotte saw Anne open her reticule for him. She looked down, her face blanched, and she stared at Charlotte.

What's wrong? Charlotte mouthed the words.

While the officer studied a map of the railroad line to pinpoint the location of the bridge, Anne edged over to let Charlotte see inside her reticule. At the bottom was a cameo brooch just like the one Mary Green had been wearing. How in the world had it ended up in Anne's reticule? The constable would search Anne's purse and find it. And the penalty for jewelry theft was prison or deportation.

Charlotte snatched the brooch and wrapped it in the handkerchief tucked in her sleeve. With her hand behind her back, she dropped it directly over the coal bucket standing next to the black potbelly stove.

A moment later, Railway Constable Burton searched Anne's reticule, sorting carefully through the bits, and then put everything back in. "Mrs. Green claimed that you ladies were very friendly to her daughter," he explained, "asking nosy questions, she said, to get close to her."

Charlotte was surprised and angry at the accusation. "Mary looked sick, but when we tried to be pleasant to her, Mrs. Green would not even let her speak."

The railway constable frowned. "I understood that you were alone with the victim, Miss Brontë."

"Well, yes," Charlotte admitted. "I told you we walked on the platform at Sheffield and talked a bit." *And I bought her some tea*, Charlotte remembered. Should she mention it? Or would Mrs. Green then accuse her of poisoning Mary's tea? When the officer said nothing, she finally asked, "May we go now? I need to buy new tickets because we have missed our connection." *And I want to put some distance between Anne and that cameo.*

"Yes, you're free to go."

As soon as they were outside, Charlotte linked arms with Anne and whispered, "When could someone have planted that brooch in your bag?"

"I have no idea."

"Did you leave your reticule unattended today?"

"No, I always had it with me, on my wrist or beside me on the train seat." She stopped abruptly and nearly tripped Charlotte. "Except for that accident!"

"What accident?"

"Remember when Mrs. Green screamed? You raced over the footbridge back to the platform we'd arrived on. I couldn't keep up with you, and everyone on the platform was running helter-skelter."

"Yes, but what—" And then Charlotte remembered. "A guard knocked you down!"

"No, he hooked my reticule on his sleeve button as he ran by, and it jerked me off my feet. My reticule went flying, but he picked it up for me."

"While planting the cameo brooch on you," Charlotte said, breathing rapidly.

Anne eyed her dubiously. "Would a train guard plant stolen jewelry on me?"

Charlotte said nothing. Newspapers reported that much of the theft on trains was actually perpetrated by railroad staff. So it could have been a guard, one who helped load the luggage for the Greens. If he'd stolen Mary's belongings, and then Mrs. Green started screaming, he couldn't afford to have the brooch discovered on him. Maybe he had planted it on Anne. Charlotte quickly scanned their surroundings. If that was the case, the guard would be waiting, biding his time until he could get Anne alone and take it back.

She pulled Anne closer. "Don't leave my side," she said. "Try to remember more details about that guard. Could you identify him?"

"I doubt it. He was clean-shaven, but most of them are."

"Let's ask the head porter." Charlotte marched up to the heavyset man overseeing the luggage and described the young guard they sought. "Slender, not much out of his teenage years probably."

The head porter frowned. "No idea who you mean. Must have come up on a London train. He's not a Leeds guard." He moved off without another word, his every movement broadcasting what a busy and important man he was.

Well, we don't need that porter's help. Charlotte and Anne would keep their eyes open and sharp, there at Leeds and as they took the train home. If Anne spotted the young guard again, Charlotte would knock him flat if she had to. She had some questions, and she was getting desperate for answers.

8

Cabot Falls, Vermont
Present Day

The home economics students were enthusiastic on Monday during the candy-making sessions as they learned to melt chocolate in double boilers and create chocolate molds. The heart-shaped and round molds would be used during the week to make multicolored layered candies and cream-filled candies. Sofia was glad she'd had to focus so intently on the teaching that day. Candy had to be watched closely, and it was so easy—and expensive—to ruin a batch.

She'd received a note during her last class from Pat Cooper, asking Sofia to join her in the school library.

Sofia still felt odd about Pat volunteering for the tutoring program in order to do what she called her "undercover work." But if she'd managed to uncover something helpful, Sofia would be glad to hear about it.

It was now a whole week since Jim had been suspended. How she had looked forward to coming to school with Jim for these two weeks, teaching in the same building, getting to know his coworkers.

It hadn't turned out like that at all.

Hurrying to the library, Sofia pushed open the glass double doors. Off to the right was the research room, and off to the left was the computer lab. Directly ahead, seated at a round table with a stack of handouts she was stapling was Pat, wearing her SHiPS Volunteer badge.

Sofia pulled out a chair. "I got your note."

"Good." Pat glanced around the room and lowered her voice. "I talked to Jim this morning before coming to school. He was outside working on the yard."

Sofia raised an eyebrow.

"Jim told me, after I prodded him a bit, that he remembered something odd happening at school two weeks ago."

"Really?" Sofia bristled. *Why didn't he tell me instead of Pat?*

"I learned my technique from watching crime shows. You know, how to ask questions to evoke a person's memory. I got him to think about various ways those perps might have gotten ahold of his grades to change them."

Sofia pressed her lips together to suppress a laugh. *Pat and her perps.* "So what did he remember?"

"He said he got a phone call telling him to come to the parking lot, something about his car lights being left on. He ran down there between classes, but no one was there, and his car was fine."

Sofia frowned. "I'm missing the significance of this, I'm afraid."

"He'd been working on putting together a math test when the call came. Someone wanted him out of the way."

"Was his test taken? How odd that he didn't think to report this."

"No, that's just it. Nothing was taken. Nothing looked disturbed at all."

"Then I don't see . . ."

Pat grabbed her wrist. "One thing I noticed this week is this: kids and adults these days take photos of everything with their phones. Selfies, photos of their friends and pets, you name it."

Sofia's eyes widened. "Of course. Someone could have seen Jim working on the test, called him away from the room, and then taken photos of the test pages on their phone."

"I know it doesn't explain getting into his computer and changing grades, but I'm working on that too." Pat hit the stapler hard and tossed the handout on her growing stack. "I want you to ask Jim for a list of students whose grades were changed so I can investigate. It's just like I thought. No matter where I'm working, I'm invisible because I'm old. Kids talk openly as if I have no ears."

"Jim did mention that three of the grades were changed for some athletes," Sofia said. "It could be those kids."

"Or their coaches," Pat said. "It's the athletic coaches—or the kids' parents—who care the most about having a winning season with lots of stars on the team. None of the teams' coaches—track, baseball, golf, tennis—will want their stars suspended from the team because of grades." She grimaced. "Or to have them take precious time away from practice to actually study."

Sofia nodded in admiration. While she'd thought Pat's idea of working undercover as a tutor had been melodramatic, she might have to revise her opinion.

"You need a ride home?" Sofia asked.

"No, I've got my car, and I'm not done yet. Thanks!"

On the way out of the building, Sofia passed the teachers' lounge and remembered that she'd left her umbrella there the week before. She pushed open the door and walked in on a discussion about the suspended teachers.

"—as well as who's guilty," the band teacher said.

The literature teacher nodded. "The pressure lately has increased to the point that anyone would buckle." She turned to Sofia. "Not everyone is judging Jim. We understand the pressure."

Sofia frowned. "What do you mean?"

The band teacher took a swig of his soda. "Just that we sympathize with whoever caved in and changed grades, whether it was Jim or not."

Sofia felt the heat rise in her face, but she said nothing.

The literature teacher spread her hands wide. "Pressure for good grades is rampant now, both pressure on the students and pressure by administrators on teachers to 'fix' or 'adjust up' their students' grades so they pass."

Sofia nearly choked. "But why would administrators encourage cheating?"

"So students qualify for scholarships to prestigious colleges, for one thing, and the high school receives more government money when everyone's grades are higher."

Sofia hadn't known that, but their words made her feel like exploding.

"Jim would never give in to pressure of any kind to fix grades," she said, her voice like steel.

"We're not accusing anyone," the band teacher hastened to say. "But we would understand if Jim—or whoever—gave in to the pressure."

"Well, *I* wouldn't understand," Sofia snapped, grabbing her umbrella.

She stormed down the hallway. While she didn't want Jim to be judged by his coworkers, she didn't want any of them "understanding" why he fixed grades either!

She'd get the list of names Pat wanted, and she'd get it tonight.

Yorkshire, England
July 1848

Patting Anne's trembling arm, Charlotte headed to the ticket counter. Her youngest sister was frail, and the heat of midday was taking its toll. Charlotte needed to get her home. She got in line behind an extremely tall man.

Their train to Keighley had left twenty minutes ago, and she wondered if James Thomas had been on that train. She hoped not. She wanted a chance to follow him when they arrived at Keighley. Something about the bogus home address he'd given made her think: *If he deliberately gave the railway constable a false address, what else did he lie about?*

A train whistle sounded up the line, and a few seconds later, an engine appeared in the distance. It puffed clouds of smoke into the air and rattled along toward them at a slowly diminishing speed. It eventually reached the station and drew up to a halt in front of them. Passengers waited to board the train while several people on it alighted.

Why is the ticket line so slow? Charlotte fumed. She felt like they'd been at the Leeds station for days instead of hours. They were nearly to the front of the line before Charlotte noticed Mr. Muttonchops at the ticket window. Mr. Smithwick asked for the next fare to London.

"That's odd," Charlotte whispered. "He just got to Leeds. Why turn right around and go back to London without doing any insurance business in the city?" What about Mary's death could have affected his plans so much?

Charlotte purchased their tickets to Keighley and put the change in her reticule.

"Miss Charlotte Brontë! Miss Anne Brontë!"

Charlotte whipped around, startled by their names spoken so publicly. It was Railway Constable Burton again. Anne clutched Charlotte's arm, and Charlotte felt her trembling grip through her sleeve. She and Anne stepped to the side to await the officer.

"Yes?" Charlotte forced a confidence into her voice that belied her true feelings. *What now?* Had he already found the cameo in the coal bucket? Or unbeknownst to Mary, had Mrs. Green been aware of the love letters and now realized they also were missing? Charlotte willed herself to keep her face blank.

"Step over here, please," he said grimly. "Your presence is still required here after all."

"Our train leaves in fifteen minutes," Charlotte protested.

"You may not be on it," Railway Constable Burton replied.

"We can't afford to keep buying new train tickets!" Charlotte said. "You said we were free to leave."

"That was before the stationmaster banked his stove to make tea and discovered this"—he opened his palm to reveal the cameo brooch—"wrapped in a handkerchief in the coal bucket." He paused. "Right by where you stood."

Charlotte felt physically ill. She'd assumed they bought tea from the vendor on hot summer days instead of building a fire in the stove. At least she hadn't used a monogrammed handkerchief.

"Are you accusing us of something?" Charlotte demanded, forcing righteous indignation into her voice. "That handkerchief could belong to anyone." She glared at the railway constable, knowing instinctively that she didn't dare show any weakness.

He paused. "I'm not accusing *you* of anything, but someone has accused your sister."

"Me?" Anne squeaked.

Fear flashed through Charlotte before astonishment took over. "Who accused Anne?"

"Come with me." Stepping between the sisters, he strode back to the stationmaster's office and ushered them inside. There, the stationmaster waited with an impatient and irate Celia May. *She's dropped the flirting and eyelash fluttering,* Charlotte noted. Apparently it didn't work its magic on the stationmaster the way it had on the susceptible James Thomas. Or was Celia angry because she'd been accused of theft too?

Charlotte glanced around at a noise. Was someone waiting in the back office to accuse them?

Railway Constable Burton blocked the exit. "I've requested that you ladies come back after the stationmaster discovered this cameo hidden in the coal bucket. Someone obviously dumped it when you learned that your purses were to be searched."

Charlotte frowned. "But you said someone had accused my sister of the theft. Where is that person?" She glanced at the closed door marked *Private*. "We have a right to face the accuser."

The officer cleared his throat. "Your sister's accuser is already in this room." He turned to Celia May. "Miss May claims that she witnessed your sister leaning over Mary Green just before she was found dead in the carriage."

"What?" Charlotte exclaimed. "Anne was never in the Greens' carriage at all!"

"Yes she was," Celia said. "I came back to look for a fan I thought I'd dropped in the carriage, and she was there, leaning inside right beside Miss Green. I found my fan outside the carriage, picked it up, and left." She looked at Anne. "I don't suppose you even saw me, but I decided the police should know."

Charlotte whirled around to the railway constable. "She's lying. I don't know why, perhaps to cover her own theft, but my sister was never near the Greens' carriage."

Anne's soft-spoken voice cut through the room. "Yes I was."

"What?" Charlotte whirled around. "No you weren't. I was with you all the time."

"Except when you left to ask a guard to clean up some broken glass you'd stepped in, remember?"

It came back to Charlotte in a flash. Yes, she had done that while Mrs. Green was giving orders to the poor porter. And Celia May had departed the Greens' carriage before then.

Anne was visibly shaking. "I did stop at the carriage to tell

Miss Green I hoped she was well soon. She was sleeping, I assumed, so I didn't bother her."

The railway constable's question was sharp. "Was she wearing the cameo when you looked in on her?"

Anne's eyes glistened. "I didn't notice. I'm sorry."

"Well," he said, "both Miss May and Mrs. Green *did* notice. They both swear that Mary Green was wearing her cameo when the train pulled into Leeds. But when her body was removed, the cameo was missing."

His somber words hung in the air, menacing and heavy. Charlotte's head spun, and she feared she might faint. Oh, why had she ever convinced Anne to go with her to London? Her sister had wanted to stay quietly and safely at home with her books and writing and gardening.

What horror have I dragged her into?

9

Cabot Falls, Vermont
Present Day

$\mathcal{S}$ofia was nearly home before she remembered that she'd promised Marla to stop by the public library after school. She dropped the kids off at home with a message for Jim, then headed downtown. Frankly, after her emotional run-in with the two teachers in the lounge, it was probably better that she get some detox time before her evening with Jim.

The minute she walked into the library, she spotted Marla at the checkout desk with a woman and two small girls. Looking animated, Marla motioned for Sofia to go to her office.

Marla joined her a minute later. "I think you might be on to something," she said without preliminary. "I started here." She pulled Sofia over to her side of the desktop computer. "There's a wealth of information at the Brontë Parsonage Museum website where I started. They have pictures of Charlotte's clothes and descriptions."

"You think I'm right, then?" Sofia asked.

"I don't know, of course," Marla said, "but I also opened links to some intriguing information about where and when paisley material was made. Sofia, you've done well in the past by trusting your instincts. We can start there anyway." She winked. "And you don't have to tell Rosa yet."

Sofia laughed and pulled up a chair. Soon, she was engrossed in reading about and studying photos of the Brontë sisters' home. Marla was right about the clothing. She took special interest in the paisley patterned items, the shawls and fichus. The earliest examples of British shawls showed garments made by weavers in Spitalfields, Norwich, Edinburgh, and *Paisley.*

"Look at this one, Marla."

Heads together, they studied a paisley print shawl, a long rectangular shape with paisley teardrop patterns in long rows. It was in shades of lighter and darker green, with a different kind of embroidery on the edges. "I think that's herringbone," Marla said.

"My lavender square has featherstitch embroidery, but I assumed it was added on when it was pieced. Maybe not." She read on. "This didn't belong to Charlotte Brontë though. It's just typical of the period in England. Are there photos of Charlotte's shawls somewhere?"

"Yes, here." Marla clicked a link. "It says that she had a fine gray cashmere shawl, and on Sundays she wore a white one."

Sofia sat back, disappointed. "But no lavender paisley."

"That doesn't mean she didn't own one. Not everything in the museum is on the website, I don't imagine. Besides, if it was cut up as part of your quilt, they wouldn't display the tattered remnants of it."

"That's true." Sofia glanced at the wall clock and gasped. "Have I really been here an hour?" She pushed her chair back. "Thank you for this wonderful break, but I need to get home and make supper and get ready for tomorrow. We're making candies filled with truffle and peanut butter filling."

And, she thought, *I have one more thing to do. I must get the list of Jim's students whose grades were fixed to give my eighty-year-old undercover neighbor.* The idea would sound amusing to anyone she told, but in fact, it was anything but funny.

Yorkshire, England
July 1848

The police constable's accusation hung heavy in the room, and Charlotte feared her sister was going to faint. Charlotte gave a quick shake of her head, and her mind cleared. "The brooch was planted on Anne, and we know when."

Railway Constable Burton froze. "Then you admit that your sister had the cameo in her possession?"

Charlotte hesitated, wishing with every fiber in her being that she could take the words back. It was too late now. She nodded slowly.

Anne cleared her throat. "I didn't know I had it until I opened my reticule for you to search. Truly, I didn't!" Her voice shook. "But I think I know when it came into my possession."

In tones so quiet that the constable had to lean close to hear, Anne gave a halting account of being run into by a guard, having items spill out of her reticule, having the young guard pick it all up and return her purse when helping her to her feet. "The brooch must have been added to my reticule at that point."

"And can you identify this train guard?" he asked.

"He was young. No mustache or beard. Very lean."

"It shouldn't be hard to find this guard," the railway constable said, turning to the stationmaster. "Right?"

"It might be." He pointed to the train schedules on the wall. "You'll need to check all the trains that passed through this morning, going both ways."

The officer tried to hide his exasperation and failed. "Why?"

"No one of that description works out of our Leeds station."

The railway constable hit his truncheon on his leg, and Charlotte wondered how bruised he was at the end of a frustrating day. He pointed with his stick at both sisters. "It's unfortunate, but I'm afraid that you will need to stay in Leeds until we clear this up."

"No, we don't have to," Charlotte snapped. "Our train leaves in five minutes."

"Would you prefer to have me take your sister to the local jail until we sort it out?"

Anne gasped. "Charlotte!"

Charlotte glared at the railway constable. "Fine. We'll stay."

"Good. If you leave the station, first tell me where you're going."

Charlotte didn't reply. She took Anne's arm and left the stationmaster's office. She was fuming by the time they arrived at the vendor's and ordered tea and biscuits. "I could throttle Miss Celia May," she said, settling on a bench out of the sun. "She had no business accusing you."

"It's not her fault, Charlotte. She only told the truth about what she saw. She couldn't know that I only peeked in and never even spoke to Mary." She stared straight ahead, as if in a trance, her biscuit untouched and her tea growing cold.

Charlotte was anxious about the color of Anne's skin. She was paler than usual, with a sheen of perspiration on her forehead. "Eat," Charlotte encouraged her. "Keep up your strength." *Because,* Charlotte added silently, *the only way we can prove your innocence is to find the person responsible for the theft ourselves.*

But how could they do that? Even if they were free to leave Leeds, they could never track down every train that had passed through that morning to find the young guard.

Despite her own roiling stomach, Charlotte sipped her sugary tea until she sensed a surge of energy. She'd have to prove Anne's innocence another way. But how?

And then she knew. She patted her abdomen and the secret pocket of letters. She'd start there, and she couldn't wait to read them until the ride home. Perhaps an important clue was hidden in the letters she'd had no chance to read.

Charlotte desperately hoped so, for Anne's sake. And yes, for Mary Green's sake too, a girl who had died decades before her time.

"I need to read the rest of Mary's letters," Charlotte said.

She sketched out her plan, and they went into action. First, Charlotte visited the lavatory and retrieved the letters from the secret pocket. Then they found Railway Constable Burton and told him they wanted to walk back to St. John's. He raised an eyebrow in disbelief.

"To pray," Anne said simply.

Charlotte kept a perfectly placid look on her face but said nothing. Anne fully intended to pray while Charlotte read the letters.

In ten minutes, they'd skirted puddles and soggy grass in the graveyard and found a quiet corner inside at the back of the church. The nave was deserted at the moment, which suited Charlotte perfectly. Anne knelt at the altar, and that would explain their presence in case the vicar returned after lunch.

Charlotte shook off her guilt at invading Mary's privacy and removed the first letter from its envelope. If Mary was murdered—and Charlotte still believed she was—finding the young guard who framed Anne could lead to the man who murdered Mary.

Ignoring the cold and the damp in the old church, Charlotte studied the remaining three letters for clues she could follow. Each letter was signed with the initials N.S. Two of them stressed the need for privacy until they were ready to plead their case to Mary's parents. Charlotte wished she could read the letters Mary had written to N.S. Then she could unravel his ambiguous references to things she must have asked. Mostly, he urged her to be patient.

One letter referred to Scarborough and his desire to go back to the seaside. "But alone with you, dear Mary, instead of surrounded by excited children." A second letter asked about her mother's temperance duties and when Mary might be home alone.

The last envelope held a photograph, which Charlotte examined eagerly. It was of an embracing couple, and Mary's face looked overjoyed. But the young man, dressed in a worn-looking coat and square-toed boots, was facing away. Had it been taken on one of the Band of Hope excursions? If so, who had taken the photo?

The letters hadn't really revealed anything new, and Charlotte felt a profound sense of disappointment bordering on despair. And then a shocking thought struck her, an idea so startling that her foot jerked and she kicked the pew in front of her.

Could N.S. be the killer?

Charlotte blinked and sat very still, letting her astonishing thought fragments gather.

N.S. stressed the vital importance of keeping his identity a secret. Had he harbored hidden reasons for making sure Mary never mentioned him to her family? Had Mary been taken in by a confidence man? Did N.S. intend to rob her family after Mary invited him there when she was alone?

In fact, was N.S. breaking into their home *right now*, while Mr. Green was in France and Mrs. Green was distraught at the railway station?

Or had the person who searched Mary's reticule and luggage been N.S. hunting for the photo of them together? It would be useful for blackmailing the parents. It was certainly not the way the Greens would expect their compliant and dutiful young daughter to behave in public—and with a commoner. They would likely pay a significant amount of money to keep that photo out of the hands of the press, especially now with Mary's death. They wouldn't want her memory besmirched.

Charlotte glanced up at the sound of Anne's footsteps. She showed her the photo.

"Doesn't she look happy?" Anne asked wistfully. "Who could have taken this?"

"Few people other than the press have access to cameras," Charlotte said. "Maybe a reporter took it. Mary said their picture was in the London paper along with their children's groups. This private one was no doubt taken without permission."

Charlotte slipped the photo back into the envelope and the letters into her travel luggage. Perhaps Mary was being blackmailed with the photo, but it was unlikely. She wouldn't have access to the sums of money needed to satisfy a blackmailer. No, this photo was surely intended for blackmailing her father, the banker. He would pay.

He still might have to, she thought, if there were more photos in existence besides this one. But in truth, today, he'd already paid the ultimate price.

Charlotte pondered their next steps as they walked back to the train station. How could she find out about the photo? She needed to know who had taken it and how it came to be in N.S.'s possession to give to Mary. Anne had no ideas.

"What about our publisher?" Charlotte asked. "He might know how to find out."

"Mr. Smith?" Anne asked doubtfully.

They walked into the train station waiting room as Charlotte explained. "I'll ask Mr. Smith or Mr. Elder to check the newspaper archives and see who took photos for the Band of Hope trips, especially Mary Green's group." Charlotte sat down immediately to write her letter.

"If you have space at the end," Anne said, "ask him about the opera too. Mr. Thomas said he saw Jenny Lind perform last night."

"Good idea." Charlotte paused, her pencil poised over her paper. "I'll ask if he can help with anything on Edward Smithwick too." She described in her letter how he'd hurried back to London after Mary died instead of continuing on with his insurance calls, plus how he'd pretended not to know the Greens, even though Anne had heard him talking to Mary's mother.

Charlotte wrote hurriedly, grateful that she had paper with her. She wondered if all ladies carried paper and pencils in their reticules, or just the Brontë sisters. "There. Done. I asked Mr. Smith to send his reply to Haworth."

"Do you truly believe they will let us go home?" Hope battled with fear in Anne's voice.

"Two spinster ladies are hardly dangerous criminals unsafe to be let loose in society." Charlotte laughed abruptly. "If he tries to keep us, Papa will storm in here to retrieve us. I wouldn't want to be in Railway Constable Burton's shoes if that happens."

Charlotte bought a stamp from the vendor and posted her letter. With any luck, it would be on the next royal mail car leaving Leeds and get to London later that night.

10

Cabot Falls, Vermont
Present Day

*B*efore school Tuesday morning, Sofia gave Pat the list of four names of Jim's students whose grades were changed. Three were star athletes for three Cabot Falls High School varsity teams: baseball, track, and golf.

"I'll get on it," Pat said. "I only have two tutoring periods today, so I'll just float around the building after that."

"Be careful," Sofia said. "You taught here a long time, so you may not be as invisible as you think."

A shadow passed briefly across Pat's face. "Even though it's only been eight years since I retired, very few of my colleagues are still here. It's sad." She straightened then. "But don't you worry. Pat Cooper is on the case."

Sofia nodded her appreciation, then hoisted to her hip a box of candy supplies for the day's cooking classes. At noon, after three periods, Sofia headed to the restroom down the hall to wash the unsalted butter and natural peanut butter off her hands. When she stepped inside, the restroom door closed behind her with a thud.

She whirled around and saw with relief that it was Pat. She was leaning against the door to keep others out.

"What's going on?" Sofia watched her in the mirror above the sink as she washed.

"Are you free now?"

"I've got a lunch period."

"Good. You need to come with me. *Now*."

Sofia shook her dripping hands. "Go where? What's going on?"

"I trailed after the boys, those athletes on the list you gave me. One of them, Jason Graves, was just summoned over the intercom in the cafeteria where I was eating lunch."

"Summoned to go where?"

"Coach Harrison's athletic office. The coach and Jason's dad were meeting him there, according to what I overheard."

"What do you want me to do?" Sofia asked, leery of where the conversation was headed.

"Come with me right now. I want a witness."

"To what?"

"Don't you see? They're all in it together: the coach, the rich parent, the star athlete who can't keep his grades high enough to stay on the team."

Sofia thought about it, and while Pat's ideas normally seemed a little farfetched, this one made an awful lot of sense. She tossed the paper towel into the trash. "Let's go. But I have to be back to set up my next class in twenty minutes."

Trying to appear as if they were just out for a friendly stroll, Sofia and Pat left the building by the back door and headed down to the athletic field. Sofia didn't see anyone, but Pat marched along like a drill sergeant, determinedly making a beeline for the coach's office housed in the green cement-block building by the football field. The front half of the building facing the field was a concession stand, while the door to the back half was the entrance to Coach Harrison's office.

As they crossed the gravel parking area, Pat and Sofia slowed down as if by mutual consent to cut the noise. They crept near the office door, which was ajar by a couple of inches.

Nothing.

Sofia looked at Pat and lifted both shoulders. Pat kept listening, her ear near the door. Suddenly Sofia made out voices, yet they sounded muffled and far away. Where were they coming from?

Sofia grabbed Pat's arm, put a finger to her lips, and pointed around to the far side by the concession stand. She only heard two voices, both adults. Was Jason with them yet? Sofia glanced over her shoulder. Or was the baseball player coming up behind them, ready to sound the alarm and give them away?

No one was in sight behind them, so Sofia and Pat crept forward. Sofia peeked around the first corner of the cement-block building.

No one.

She motioned Pat to follow her, and they took several more steps. Then, out of the breeze, Sofia could hear perfectly.

"So the problem is straightened out?" asked a deep voice.

"I was assured that a second payment would cover it."

The first voice asked, "Have you seen your midterm report yet?"

A younger voice answered then. "None of my grades were below a B–."

One of the older men chuckled. "If your father pays enough, you just might win a full-ride scholarship to State."

"Yeah. Maybe." There was a pause. "What about finals? Do I have to take them?"

A laugh. "Depends on what your dad wants to pay, from what I've heard."

The crunching of gravel startled Sofia, and she realized the three men were heading their way. *Oh, please,* Sofia thought, *go into the coach's office. Don't come around the building yet.*

Sofia placed a finger to her lips, then forcefully turned Pat around. They headed back quickly and quietly to the school.

She had no illusions about the chances she and an older woman would have against two grown men and a teenage athlete.

Yorkshire, England
July 1848

After Charlotte posted the letter to the publisher, she turned to Anne. "Would you like to stroll with me on the platform?"

Anne fanned herself and glanced at the glaring sun now overhead. "I will rest in the shade, if you do not mind."

"Anne, look." Charlotte nodded toward an exit.

A small man dressed in gray with protruding teeth hurried up to Edward Smithwick, his hand extended. "Ned! Good to see you." He looked like an agreeable mouse.

"I thought Mr. Smithwick was going back to London," Anne said.

"His ticket must be for a later time." Charlotte set her valise next to Anne's feet. "You rest here in the shade. I won't go far, but I think better on my feet."

It had always been that way. She might have great difficulty writing a scene in her novel, but if she paced around the dining room table, it loosened something in her. And if her sisters were there to discuss ideas with, even better. The words would flow like her favorite waterfall on the moors.

Charlotte set off down the platform, oblivious to the heat or the rushing passengers around her. What should she do next? There must be something. She had to clear Anne of suspicion.

And after seeing Mary's photo in which she was so clearly happy, she had to get to the bottom of her death. She certainly hadn't killed herself. And Charlotte would never believe that Mary had accidentally taken an overdose of a medicine she hated to take.

Head down, she walked south on the platform, beyond the green-and-black engine at the front of the train. And then, unexpectedly, recent words came back to her. When calling a greeting, Mr. Smithwick's friend had said 'Ned,' the nickname for Edward. *Ned Smithwick!* Could he be the mysterious N.S. of the love letters? But would Mary fall in love with him? It seemed doubtful, but after he pretended not to have spoken to the Greens, she had to follow up on him. Charlotte wished she could tell the railway constable, but then she would have to admit to taking evidence off the victim.

She pivoted on her heel and started back down the platform the way she had come, still deep in thought. She nodded to the engineer and fireman stoking the coal fire. She passed empty carriages, both first and second class, then a bright-red mail coach, and finally a guard's van.

She stopped abruptly. A guard's van! Why hadn't she thought of that before? If the guard who knocked Anne down and planted the cameo in her reticule wanted to hide, where better than in the guard van at the end of the train?

Charlotte grabbed the door handle of the van and, without knocking, jerked it open. It took a moment for her eyes to adjust to the dim interior. Then she spotted a young guard sitting on a crate at the rear of the car. He jumped up, but Charlotte blocked the doorway.

"Yes?" He wiped a hand across his face. "Can I help you?"

Charlotte advanced slowly, peering closely at the guard. He was definitely young, with horn-rimmed glasses that looked foggy.

Not clean-shaven, though. His thin mustache could have been a dirty upper lip. Charlotte frowned. "I remember you," she said. "You were kind to Mary Green earlier."

He swallowed hard, his pronounced Adam's apple bobbing up and down. He didn't look Charlotte in the eye, but his own were puffy looking.

Charlotte started to touch his arm, then pulled back. "Are you quite all right?"

The guard sniffed and muttered, "I have a cold."

"I don't think so," Charlotte said softly. "You're obviously very upset about something." She paused, and her eyes opened wide. "Or some*one*." She touched his arm then. "Why? Who are you?"

His shoulders stiffened, then suddenly slumped further. "Nic Strada."

And then, one after another, pieces dropped into place. *N.S.!* No wonder he'd stopped to ask if Mary was all right and to offer his help. He loved her! He helped escort the Band of Hope children on seaside excursions because he already worked on the train as a guard. And he didn't have a cold. He'd hidden in the back of the guard van, weeping because the girl he loved was dead.

"I am so very sorry," Charlotte said. "You must be the young man Mary told me about."

He jerked away from her. With great visible effort, he got his emotions under control. "What are you talking about?"

"Mary Green, who loved you." She knew she was right when tears sprang to his eyes again. "Mary told me about the trips to the seaside and getting your picture taken with the children for the London paper." Charlotte hesitated. She knew she was intruding on this young man's grief, but she might not get another chance to question him. "Do you live in London?"

He wiped his sleeve across his eyes and nodded. "That's where my Band of Hope children live. They're all under ten and love to ride the train."

"And you and Mary hoped to have a future together?" Charlotte asked.

"I hoped. Mary planned." A ghost of a smile crossed his face. "She was much surer than I was that she could persuade her parents to let us marry." He laughed, but there was no humor in it. "Can you see a bank president allowing his only daughter to marry a train guard?"

Charlotte didn't answer. If Mrs. Green was any indication, she would have to agree with the despondent young man. "And so the secrecy?" she asked.

"Mary didn't agree with me, but it had to be a secret, perhaps for a very long time." The young man's voice was heavy with misery. "Now it will be a secret forever."

Charlotte wondered if that was possible. She was trying to determine how to steer the conversation around to the missing guard who planted Mary's brooch on Anne when the van's doorway was abruptly darkened. Charlotte swung around. A tall man's shadow blocked the sunlight, and she couldn't see his face.

But she recognized his voice.

"Excuse me for interrupting," Railway Constable Burton said slowly, "but I want to be part of this conversation." He stepped in, allowing the sunlight to again fill the guard van. "Don't stop. What I heard was very interesting. You had great plans with this wealthy young girl. Repeat that part about keeping your relationship a secret, but Miss Green didn't agree."

Nic swallowed over and over, licked his lips, but said nothing.

The constable's voice grew a steel edge. "What did you decide to do to Mary since she wanted to tell the world about you? Did you kill her because you had other plans, either to rob her or blackmail her father?"

"No! It wasn't like that!" Nic looked wildly from the railway constable to Charlotte and back to the constable. "I would never hurt Mary!"

"They truly loved each other," Charlotte said, remembering the stolen love letters.

"Come, come, Miss Brontë," the officer said. "This isn't *Romeo and Juliet*, the star-crossed lovers. It's not even one of *your* novels. This is real life. He may have convinced Mary Green that he loved her, but this guard is a con man."

"I'm not!" Nic cried. "I loved Mary!"

"Mary's money, you mean," the railway constable said, lightly swinging his painted wood truncheon. "Come along, son. I have some official questions for you."

Sick at heart, Charlotte followed the officer and Nic Strada as the railway constable marched the young man to the station-master's office. She wondered if, at the very least, the young guard would get fired. Had he done anything against company rules, meeting Mary clandestinely when on the train? Surely not. Even if he lost his job, Charlotte wasn't sure the young man would care right now, perhaps not for a long time. He was grief-stricken over Mary's death. She was sure about that.

And although Ned Smithwick wasn't the N.S. of the letters to Mary, it didn't clear his name. His story had holes in it, and he'd definitely lied about not having met Mr. and Mrs. Green at some point in the past.

When the constable disappeared inside the stationmaster's office with Nic, Charlotte found Anne in the cooler ladies' waiting room. Her ball of yarn rested in her lap, fingers moving swiftly, lips moving silently. Trust Anne to be praying. Papa would be pleased if he could see her.

Charlotte took an empty seat next to her sister and filled her in on what had happened in the guard van. "I feel so guilty," she said. "I don't believe Nic Strada is Mary's killer, despite what the railway constable thinks."

Ten minutes later, another train screeched to a stop on the farther platform, and Railway Constable Burton dashed past, practically running for the footbridge over the tracks. "I wonder what the emergency is now," Charlotte said.

He disappeared from sight for a moment, then reappeared on the other platform, disappearing again behind the newly arrived train. Within a minute, Charlotte spotted the constable coming back, only he wasn't alone this time. Apparently, he'd met someone coming in on the train from up north somewhere.

The man accompanying the railway constable was immaculately attired in a frock coat with tails, striped trousers, and stovepipe top hat. He marched with military precision, looking straight ahead. Who could he be? Whoever he was, his air of authority was palpable.

"Come here, Anne," Charlotte said. "Look who the constable met. Do you think it's Mr. Green, back from France?"

After crossing the footbridge and descending the stairs, the two men advanced along the platform back to the station. Up closer, the new arrival appeared to be in his middle years, but still tall and slim, dark hair nearly black, with a beak nose reminding Charlotte of goshawks that glided over the moors. As he walked, he pulled his watch from his pocket, and Charlotte could almost hear him click his tongue in irritation.

Charlotte watched until they passed from view. "They're headed for the stationmaster's office. If Mary's body is still in the private back room, then Mrs. Green is likely still there, keeping a vigil."

Anne frowned. "Could Mr. Green get back already?"

"Not unless he was already on his way home. But if it *is* him, I want to talk to him. If he has any known enemies, they need to be investigated." Charlotte gathered her things.

Anne put a restraining hand on her arm. "Stay with me, Charlotte," she implored. "Let the railway constable forget about us."

"I want him to focus on someone else too, but if that someone is Mary's young man, that will be as big a miscarriage of justice as when he pinned the thefts on you." Charlotte straightened her gloves and retied her bonnet strings. "I want to make Mr. Green understand that his daughter was probably murdered, which means there's a killer on the loose who could well strike his family again."

Ignoring Anne's protests, Charlotte left the comfort of the cooler waiting room and hurried outside. The heat of the July day hit her, and a brief wave of dizziness reminded her that she needed to eat soon.

She opened the door to the stationmaster's office and entered. Three people glanced at her, and their conversation died. Mrs. Green, her plump face streaked and blotchy, sat stiffly on a wooden chair by the private office door. Railway Constable Burton stood by a wall map of the train lines, and the other man sat bolt upright behind the stationmaster's desk, his palms down on the desktop. He'd removed his top hat, revealing a wide, high forehead. Nic was no longer there.

"Yes, Miss Brontë?" Railway Constable Burton asked.

She ignored him and spoke to the man behind the desk. "Are you Mary's father?"

He stared at her without blinking. "I am not." He stood then, towering over Charlotte. "I am Inspector Tipp of the Railroad Police, and I'm from London."

Charlotte frowned. London was south of Leeds. "You didn't

come up from London," she blurted out. "I saw you get off the train arriving from the north."

The inspector stared, his dark eyes drilling holes into her. Charlotte inwardly shrank back, heart hammering, but steadily held his gaze.

The silence was deafening.

11

Cabot Falls, Vermont
Present Day

*S*ofia could barely concentrate on her candy-making classes that afternoon as the overheard snatches of conversation by the athletic office replayed in her mind.

Someone—apparently the athlete's father—was paying to have his son's grades fixed. But the boy had said something else, something about when he took his midterms that sounded fishy.

He'd made it sound like someone else was going to take the test for him. But how would that be possible? Someone would surely notice if another person replaced him at testing time.

Or would they?

She froze in midstroke. Melted chocolate dripped off the end of her spatula.

"Mrs. Parker?" the girl with frizzy red hair asked her. "Are you all right?"

Sofia blinked. "Yes. Yes, of course." She smiled and focused on creating multicolored layered candy: red, green, and white for Christmas; lavender, yellow, and white for Easter; orange, yellow, and brown for Halloween. But in the back of her mind, she kept working on the puzzle.

And the only way she could figure out how that could be done was if the tests would be taken online, as they were sometimes. She didn't personally know how to hack into computers, especially password-protected sites like the school's, but there must be some way.

When Wynter hadn't arrived after school by the time Sofia was packed up and ready to leave, Sofia went looking for her. She found her finishing up in the library with Mr. Jeffries.

Sofia glanced at her open textbook: government. *Ugh*, Sofia thought. She'd hated that course when in high school. "If only I'd had someone like you back then," she said to the tutor, "I might have actually learned something useful."

Mr. Jeffries smiled and ducked his head. "I enjoy working with your daughter," he said. "She really applies herself."

Sofia glanced next door to the computer lab. "Say, maybe you could answer something for me."

"I will if I can."

"When students take tests online, like when they take makeup tests, is it done in the computer lab? Or does each teacher oversee an online test from the classroom?"

"I have no idea," Mr. Jeffries said. "I'm afraid I'm an old-fashioned paper person. I would ask Michael Daley, who runs the computer lab. Sometimes students work in there after school. Maybe he oversees them taking makeup tests." He gathered up his tutoring materials. "Mr. Daley is a whiz with technology. If anyone could answer your questions, he could."

Right then, the extremely tall and extremely thin Mr. Daley was surrounded by students. Plus Wynter was ready to leave. "I'll ask him tomorrow," she finally said. "My boys are waiting on me at the middle school too."

As she left the library, she glanced back at the computer lab. Was the person who'd been paid to fix grades the obvious choice? Who else would know better how to break into the school's computers and alter grades than the teacher who ran the computer lab?

Yorkshire, England
July 1848

Charlotte found the thick silence in the small office suffocating.

Inspector Tipp's words, when he finally spoke, were clipped. "I *am* from London. I finished a case in Newcastle just before receiving the message to come here."

Mrs. Green leaned forward. "I made the constable telegraph for a proper inspector. I wouldn't leave until he arrived. I want my Mary's murderer caught!"

"I will look into it," Inspector Tipp said, his gaze steady. "Miss? Did you have something to add to your statement?"

Embarrassed by her outburst, Charlotte wished she could begin again. "No . . ." She turned away from the inspector's piercing stare. "Mrs. Green, does your husband have any enemies you know about?"

"My husband has a lot of enemies," said Mrs. Green with a touch of pride beneath her anguish, "because he's a man of principle."

"Can you name anyone angry enough to retaliate by hurting your family?"

Before Mrs. Green could answer, Inspector Tipp made an angry jerking motion at Railway Constable Burton, and the constable sprang into action. He took Charlotte's arm to escort her outside. "This is official business, Miss Brontë. You have no part—"

She'd only taken two steps when Mrs. Green grabbed her hand and held on. "I want her here!" she cried. "She saw the truth about Mary's death, unlike my imbecile doctor." She tugged on Charlotte's arm until the officer let go.

Studying the hysterical woman, Charlotte was confused. Only an hour ago, the woman had wanted the Brontë sisters arrested as jewel thieves.

Mrs. Green stared up into Charlotte's face. "I do remember something! A letter came to the house a few weeks ago, but my husband wouldn't let me read it. It must have been a threat, though, because for two weeks, he wouldn't allow Mary or me to travel without a manservant accompanying us."

"Who was the letter from?" Charlotte asked, praying it wasn't Nic Strada.

"I don't know," Mrs. Green said, "but my husband would remember." She turned to the railway constable and commanded, "Telegraph my husband in Paris. He might not have left for home yet."

"I'll take care of it," Inspector Tipp said.

The distraught woman's grip on her arm would leave a bruise, Charlotte feared, but she didn't want to break her grasp. At least Mrs. Green gave them something on which to follow up, someone out there who was a threat to her family, someone to take the focus off Anne.

Charlotte moved to the door, then turned back to Inspector Tipp. "Find the guard who knocked my sister down and planted the cameo on her. If you do, I bet you'll find the man who wrote the threatening letter and also made good on his threat today." She glanced at the wall clock. If she and her sister hoped to make it to Keighley and walk to Haworth before dark, they needed to catch the next train north. "May Anne and I go home now?"

Inspector Tipp was clearly reluctant to grant her any favors. "I will be in touch about the inquest. You and your sister will need to testify," he finally said. "If either of you leave your home, I expect to be informed."

Charlotte nodded. Not leaving the area would *not* be a

problem. As far as she was concerned, once she arrived home, she never wanted to leave again. An inquest. And before that, there would be an autopsy. Poor Mrs. Green. Poor Mary.

Her gloved hand was on the doorknob when Inspector Tipp's voice stopped her cold. "We only have your sister's word for it that someone planted the jewelry on her. There is no proof for this very *convenient* story." Tipp's voice was clipped and cruel. "Who killed Mary? Some unknown person angry at her father? Some unknown guard without a motive? Or your sister, who was alone with the victim and later had the victim's jewelry in her possession?" Inspector Tipp resumed his seat at the desk and pressed the tips of his long, thin fingers together. "I have found over the years, Miss Brontë, that the most obvious solution is often the one that proves true."

Heart pounding so that she could barely breathe, Charlotte left the office to find Anne. It was her custom to share everything with her sisters, but not this. The inspector's threatening opinion would crush Anne.

Later, Charlotte waited beside Anne for the train to Keighley, nearly touching her, but she felt the gulf between them as if it were miles. She'd only told Anne they were free to go home. She couldn't burden her frail sister with the knowledge that she apparently was the inspector's primary murder suspect.

She heard the Keighley train before she saw it. When it finally steamed into sight, it belched out smoke that assaulted her lungs and squeals that assaulted her eardrums. The locomotive halted amid clouds of steam. Carriage doors opened, and passengers disembarked. Charlotte and Anne quickly climbed aboard for the last stage of their journey. For once, Charlotte was grateful that they were forced to share their carriage with three other travelers. It prevented Anne from asking questions that Charlotte couldn't—or didn't want to—answer.

When they arrived in Keighley thirty minutes later, they started out on the four miles to Haworth. Having to buy their train tickets twice had depleted their cash.

"On the way home," Charlotte said, "I want to take a short detour down Canal Road."

"Whatever for?" Anne asked, weariness heavy in her voice.

"Remember James Thomas?"

"The one looking for Celia May?"

"Yes, Mr. Chin. He mentioned living on Canal Road, but it doesn't sound right to me. It won't take long to check. You can wait at the station for me."

"No, I'll come too, so you don't get sidetracked. I want to get home before dark."

In ten minutes' time, they found Canal Road, a road only a few blocks long, and Charlotte's memory proved right. It was an industrial section, the street lined mostly with woolen mills. They were already shut down for the night. Why had James Thomas lied about where he lived? *More importantly,* Charlotte thought, *what else had he lied about?*

The gray-stoned houses of Keighley thinned out as the sisters walked the dirt road to Haworth. The first two miles were fairly level, with hills on the left and a beck flowing through the meadow on the right. Occasional farmhouses or rows of workmen's houses sat near the road; villas were half hidden by a screen of shrubs. Despite the midsummer warmth, the hills surrounding them seemed various shades of gray.

Then the road began to climb. Shrubs and hedges were replaced by stone dykes. Charlotte could see Haworth two miles away, situated on the side of a steep hill, with a background of wild and bleak moors that grew more purple as one climbed. St. Michael and All Angels Church was built at the town's highest point, at the end of a long, narrow cobblestone street.

The moors rose even higher than the church steeple.

In just under an hour, Charlotte and Anne were climbing the last cobblestone street up past the church and graveyard, through the courtyard garden, past lilac and elder bushes, to the front door of the two-story, gray-stoned parsonage. Charlotte couldn't help noticing how much more heavily Anne was leaning on her arm and how white the pinched lines around her mouth had become. The day's events had exhausted her.

Lights burned in the front windows of the sitting room, and Charlotte pushed open the front door with gratitude. It felt like they'd been gone for a week, not two days. After greeting Emily and their father, then asking about Branwell, Anne rejected the bread and tea waiting for them and retreated to her bed.

Charlotte didn't feel well herself, but not from exhaustion. All the way home, as they silently hiked the last miles, she'd gone over and over the inspector's words. She had to clear their names from all suspicion. The only thing she was guilty of was befriending a young girl. Charlotte couldn't share her fears with her family, but she had to talk to someone.

Nell! Of course. The perfect sounding board. She would write to her that very night and mail the letter immediately the next morning.

She and her dear friend Ellen Nussey—known by Charlotte as Nell—had met back in 1831 when they were both pupils at Roe Head School in Mirfield. Ellen was thirteen at the time and Charlotte was fourteen, and while Nell had been poised and beautiful even then, poor Charlotte recalled being awkward and small and never blending in. But Nell had befriended her, even taking her home for visits sometimes, and they'd written hundreds of letters back and forth since they left the school.

After Anne had gone to bed and Charlotte had given her father and Emily a brief account of their trip to London, Patrick

Brontë retrieved several newspapers from his study and spread them out on the dining room table.

"While I am sorry that you came to know the young woman who died, I did warn you about the dangers before you went to London."

"Yes, Papa," Charlotte said, hoping to waylay another lecture, "but nothing happened to Anne or me."

"You were spared, but you cannot presume upon the Almighty again. You must stay home." He shook the *Bradford Observer* before him, then held it close to his nose to make out the print. "Listen to this: 'On April 25 of this year, the boiler of a North Midland Railway locomotive exploded at Normanton, Derbyshire, scalding three people.'" He pointed at another open newspaper with a bony finger. "And the *Leeds Times* reported that on May 10 of this year, six passengers were killed and thirteen injured at Shrivenham, Berkshire, when a Great Western Railway express train ran into two wagons on the line."

"Oh, Papa," Emily said, "those are rare accidents. You know they are."

He slapped a hand down on the table. "I will tell you what is *not* rare!" He threw the first two papers on the floor and snatched up a *London Daily News*. "Listen to this article called 'Crime on the Railway.' It says that 'the expanding rail network gives criminals new opportunities to move around the country and commit crime.' What about that? A girl you met was killed. Criminals used the railroad to kill her!"

"But Papa," Charlotte said, "that argument won't work. The railway officials have been pioneers in catching criminals who use the trains. They used the telegraph to arrest someone a few years ago—1845, I think. A railway policeman was sent a telegraph, and he arrested a murderer named Tawell when he stepped off a train at Paddington."

Charlotte tried to make light of her father's concerns, but she couldn't tell him the real reason she would soon be traveling the trains again. She couldn't solve Mary's murder by staying at home, hiding in the parsonage, no matter how much she longed to lose herself in her writing and ignore the rest of the world.

And if the nasty, beak-nosed Inspector Tipp showed up on their doorstep with an arrest warrant for Anne, her father and sister would both collapse. She had to prevent that. She had dragged Anne into it by insisting she go to London with her to meet their publishers. It was up to Charlotte to clear her name.

Emily made an effort to lighten the mood. "Papa was reading *Jane Eyre* while you were away," she said, picking up a copy from a side table. "Just think. If it hadn't been for Admiral Lord Nelson, this would have been written by Charlotte Brunty!"

Charlotte smiled, grateful for the change in subject. Her sister referred to the patriotic circumstances that had resulted in their father changing his name from Brunty to Brontë as a young college man. When he'd arrived from his native Ireland to attend Cambridge, Patrick Brunty had wanted to honor his hero, Lord Nelson. Nelson had been given the title of Duke of Bronte by the king of Naples as a thank-you for Nelson restoring him to his throne in 1799. Bronte was the name of an estate in Sicily. So Patrick registered as an undergraduate at St. John's College Cambridge in 1802 in the name of Patrick Brontë.

Just then, a familiar yet frightening howl echoed from upstairs, and Patrick Brontë ran down the hall and up the stairs, his coattails flying. Charlotte followed her father up the stairs more slowly, dreading to see her brother's condition, which seemed to go downhill with each passing day. Branwell's moans gave Charlotte chills no matter how many nights she heard them.

Charlotte stopped in the doorway of the bedroom, where her father knelt beside Branwell's bed, praying for him and stroking his feverish sweating forehead. Branwell thrashed about, tangling the bedclothes, but as Patrick prayed, the thrashing lessened.

Charlotte's nose wrinkled. How she hated the smell of the sickroom and Branwell's medicine. And then, as she stood in the bedroom doorway, she was suddenly transported back to Mary Green's carriage where she'd stepped on the broken glass. The smell! It was alcohol, but it was the same kind as Branwell's medicine: laudanum, which was opium mixed with sherry. Had that broken glass outside Mary's carriage been a bottle holding laudanum? Had Mary been drugged to sleep so that a thief could steal without raising the alarm? Had that dose, coupled with medicine she'd already taken, killed her?

Moments later, Charlotte wrote to her friend in West Yorkshire, urging her to visit as soon as possible.

I tell you it's urgent, Nell. I do not exaggerate, my dear friend.

She mailed the letter the next morning. She had a reply from Moor Lane House within two days. The note was short.

I'm eager to see you on Friday. Early train is 6:44.

12

Cabot Falls, Vermont
Present Day

The next day, when Sofia talked to the computer lab teacher, Mr. Daley, she was surprised to hear that he had nothing to do with overseeing makeup tests. *Or so he says*, she thought. She wasn't sure why, but his denial didn't ring true.

"No," he said, "the teachers themselves oversee tests done online, and nearly always just one or two students are making up a test. It's done in their classroom, and the teacher is supposed to stay in the classroom while they take it." He'd rubbed his head. "Once in a while, I will set up a webcam for a special event though," he added.

"What kind of special event?"

"Oh, like where the principal wants a college representative to talk to several students or one of the career counselors is working with a small group of students."

"I don't understand," Sofia said.

"I just mean that sometimes, if a small group of students is working online, you can set up a webcam to oversee the room. It shows if anyone talks or leaves the room or is getting answers from their backpack or just talking to each other or on their phones." He shrugged. "It's technology today, a computerized baby sitter, of sorts."

"What if someone put something in front of the webcam so

it couldn't record?" Sofia asked. It sounded simple enough to her to fool a mechanical baby sitter.

"Not as easy as you'd think," Mr. Daley said. "The webcams are posted way up high, for one thing, and they move back and forth. They're hooked up to a computer. Any interference would be recorded on the computer, and the time stamp would tell us exactly when it happened."

"Oh, I see." *Sort of,* she added.

By the end of the school day, Sofia had decided to do some snooping of her own. She didn't know exactly what she was looking for, but she had a terrible sense of time running out. She would only be in the high school two more days. Their lawyer had come to the house last night to talk, and for the first time, Sofia was truly frightened. The lawyer hinted that the school was being pressured to prosecute and quickly pin the crime on someone.

Jim and the science teacher, at this point anyway, looked set up to take the blame.

Sofia had promised to take Vanessa to the local Goodwill after school to hunt for a few things she still needed for costumes and decorations for two of the play's scene changes. Before meeting her in the parking lot, Sofia took a quick walk past Lance Barton's science room. She knew he had a substitute while he was suspended, just like Jim did, but she wanted to look around his room. Maybe there were some similarities to Jim's math room, something that had made them both vulnerable to someone breaking into the school's grading system.

There had to be something. Supposedly, the school's password-protected website was unbreakable. But someone had hacked into it.

Sofia looked up and down the hall, then slipped into the science room. No one was there, although the lights were still on. She took a quick trip around the familiar room. Vanessa had had classes in here before, and Sofia remembered the various cages of rodents and lizards and snakes, as well as the white skeleton hanging from a pole. She hurried by them to the teacher's desk at the back, half-hidden behind a cabinet, like Jim's arrangement.

Sofia was leery of leaving fingerprints and wished she had gloves with her. She confined herself to looking at the computer, the stack of homework papers on how to dissect a worm, and attendance records. Then Sofia spied a grade book.

She had just reached for it when she heard footsteps in the hallway. She froze, bent over the desk, as the steps grew closer.

Oh, heavens, what if it was the substitute science teacher?

Frantically, Sofia swiveled from side to side, looking for a place to hide, then noticed the utility closet at the back of the room. She made a dash for it, squeezing into the tiny, dark closet alongside the shelves holding microscopes, empty aquariums, clean glass jars, and bags of table salt. She pulled the closet door closed but didn't let it latch, in case it automatically locked like so many of the school's doors.

Footsteps entered the room, and Sofia feared she might faint. The closet wasn't ventilated, and between her nerves and the close quarters, her temperature climbed. Sweat rolled between her shoulder blades.

Someone—whoever it was—whistled as he moved around the room. Papers were shuffled at the desk only ten feet away, and Sofia was afraid to breathe.

Please leave, she thought desperately. By now, Vanessa and Wynter would be waiting at the car for her. *What am I going to do?* She had to get out of there, but she couldn't just waltz out of the closet, give a wave, and leave.

Just then, another set of steps came down the hall. What if the teacher was waiting to have a meeting with someone, or a student was here to do some makeup work?

"Excuse me," someone said.

Sofia recognized the voice. Pat Cooper!

"I'm one of the grandparent volunteers, and I work with one of your students. Could we talk?"

"Sure, come on in," said a young man.

Sofia groaned silently. Pat was a real talker. She might be in here for an hour!

But instead, Pat said, "Could we walk and talk instead? I have a bad hip, and I've been sitting all day."

"Sure. No problem." The teacher's chair scraped back, and Sofia heard his steps cross the room as he left with Pat.

Sofia counted to ten, then eased the closet door open. She peered out, waited, and heard their voices disappearing down the hallway.

Slipping off her shoes, she raced on silent feet to the science room door and peeked out. Pat and a young man were walking down the hall to the left, so Sofia headed to the stairwell at the end of the hall to the right.

Just as she reached the stairwell, she glanced back down the hall. Pat Cooper was still walking the other way, but behind her back, she gave Sofia a thumbs-up signal.

Yorkshire, England
July 1848

Charlotte laid down Nell's letter of confirmation and picked up the second envelope from Smith, Elder, and Company. The recipient name on the envelope jolted her. It was her first letter from them addressed to her instead of Currer Bell. While having her secret revealed still made her nervous, it was in some ways a relief not to play hide-and-seek with her identity. Time would tell what price they'd pay for going public. As she had remarked to Mr. Smith and Mr. Elder, "What author would voluntarily be without the advantage of being able to walk invisibly? One is thereby enabled to keep a quiet mind."

In truth, she hadn't felt invisible or had a quiet mind since leaving London.

She ripped open the letter, eager to see what Mr. Smith had unearthed about Mary's photo, James Thomas's business in London, and Edward Smithwick.

Her buoyant hope deflated as she read.

About the photo, no luck there. Very sorry. Subject of the photo not important enough to record the photographer's name. About James Thomas: The Barber of Seville was the only play at Covent Garden when you accompanied us there. I Puritani with Jenny Lind never played there. However, Miss Lind performed it at Her Majesty's Theatre a few months ago.

On the last page, she learned something that took her breath away. Her editor had found a back copy of the *Times* showing that Smithwick had spent time in prison for threatening Mr. Green.

Eureka! Charlotte fell back in her chair. Her instincts had been right. Inspector Tipp might not be interested in the lies Thomas and Smithwick told, but she would dig further herself. It would be the only way to take the focus off Anne and Nic Strada as the suspects.

She'd begin the minute Nell arrived. In fact, on Friday morning, when Nell stepped off the train in Keighley, they'd track down James Thomas first thing. Then they could take the train to London to find out more about Smithwick and his ties to the Green family.

First, James Thomas *had* lied about being at Covent Garden. He'd probably never been at the theater at all. He could have read the name of the performances in the London newspaper. The question was, had he simply lied to impress Celia May? He had certainly seemed besotted with her. Or had he lied to give the railway constable a false reason for being on the train? One thing was sure: He had lied about living on Canal Road.

Early Friday morning, Charlotte met Nell's train in Keighley, enjoying the cool morning sunrise as she waited on the platform. Next to her sisters, Nell was her closest confidant. When the train chugged into sight and the steam cleared, Charlotte scanned the carriage windows. With grace as always, Nell alighted from the first carriage and glided over the platform to Charlotte.

They hugged briefly, and Nell stood back in obvious admiration. "You look lovely, not at all as I pictured from your frantic note."

Charlotte lifted Nell's travel bag, then took her friend's arm and steered her down the platform and out onto the street.

"Where are we going at such a speed?" Nell asked. "Your letter didn't reveal many details. Do the police really suspect Anne of theft?"

"Yes, and maybe murder." Several heads swiveled in their direction, and Charlotte lowered her voice almost to a whisper to fill her in.

Charlotte pointed their way toward the industrial district as she explained how a guard they couldn't find had planted jewelry on Anne and how Anne was seen leaning into the carriage where Mary had died. Charlotte explained her interest in James Thomas, who'd claimed to be a salesman of medical instruments or supplies living on Canal Road. "He portrayed himself as having a lot of money, and he mentioned the theater in London, but he lied about being there. And he looked rundown, not wealthy at all."

By the time they reached Canal Road, Nell was fully apprised of recent disturbing events. Charlotte stopped in front of the Armley Mills woolen mill. "This is the location James Thomas gave for his home address." She studied the front of the dirty gray stone building. "Let's go in."

They were directed upstairs to a small, second-floor office, which overlooked machine wool combers below. The supervisor, Mr. Broderick, was none too happy when they asked about James Thomas's whereabouts. "You tell me!" he spat. "Like I don't have enough trouble, dealing with wool combers going on strike last year. Thomas was among the leaders demanding higher wages from the mill owners."

"Were they successful?" Nell asked.

"Nah. Wool prices keep dropping. We had to lower the workers' wages by one farthing per pound."

Charlotte winced. She knew from the cottage combers in Haworth that a reduction even this small inflicted a hardship upon the poor weaver or comber. "So Mr. Thomas is not in the mill today?"

He clamped down hard on his unlit cigar. "No. He never showed up today."

"I must speak to him," Charlotte said. "It's urgent. Can you give me his home address?"

Mr. Broderick nodded. "And if you see him, tell him to get back here today or he's fired."

They left, but Charlotte didn't take the shortest route to Thomas's home. She didn't want him to spot her coming down the street and run. On the way, she made liberal use of back gardens, alleyways, side streets, even a tunnel.

"Charlotte," Nell said, "do you know where you're going?"

"I know Keighley almost as well as I know Haworth," Charlotte said. "We'll arrive at his home through a rear alley. Liars are very slippery fellows, and I don't want him slithering away."

To double-check her directions, Charlotte stopped to ask a woman sitting on a stool outside a door, bouncing a baby on her knee. From a distance, she looked quite old. Up close, though, Charlotte realized that she was barely out of her twenties. It was the rounded shoulders and air of weariness that added years to her. She looked up at them with dull eyes and answered Charlotte's request for directions with a tired nod in a westerly direction.

Without comment, Nell withdrew her handkerchief from her sleeve and pressed it against her nose. Charlotte didn't blame her. The cramped buildings in this part of the city, with their outside pumps and public outhouses, were an assault on the nose. When they found the address of James Thomas, Charlotte knocked on the door, waited, then knocked again, harder. Noise from the interior let her know a family with children was inside.

A woman answered, her look wary. "Mrs. Thomas?" Charlotte asked.

"Maybe." The woman's voice was thick with suspicion. Short and thin, her plain face looked harassed. "Who are you?" She raked a rough, reddened hand back through her straw-like hair.

"I met your husband on the train from London this week, and I need to talk to him."

The woman froze, and the noise of many children in the background quieted. Finally, she stepped back, allowing Charlotte and Nell to enter.

Moving into the cramped room, Charlotte forced herself to breathe normally. This was not the home of a man who regularly went to the opera in London. Water heated in a pot over the fireplace, and a tin bath waited in the corner. The peeling, molding wallpaper had once shown pretty pink roses. Wet laundry hung from a rope strung across the room. One corner held a bed with a rumpled quilt. Another corner near a closet door was set up for wool combing.

Charlotte felt silly for asking, fairly sure that this apartment had only one room, but she had to know. "Is your husband home?"

"No." She squinted at Charlotte. "Did he borrow money from you?"

"Good heavens, no."

"Because if he did, he can pay it back real soon."

An older boy spoke up. "Papa will have lots of money soon!"

Charlotte glanced at Nell. How could that be if he wasn't bothering to show up for work? Could it be money from stealing jewelry from travelers on the trains?

"Young Robert's right." Mrs. Thomas stood a bit taller. "My husband's mum in Liverpool died, and he gets his inheritance soon." She moved to the front door. "I will tell James you called."

Charlotte had noticed two of the four children sneaking glances at the closet door in the corner. Was James Thomas home but hiding? Mrs. Thomas seemed eager to have them leave. Charlotte moved toward the closet door, lifted aside a little girl with stringy hair, and yanked open the door. The dark closet was crammed with wooden boxes and kindling. Charlotte wished she had a candle. She tried to peer behind the boxes but couldn't see.

"Stop!" Mrs. Thomas called. "Don't!"

But Charlotte yanked a box aside, stepped over some wood, and plunged farther into the closet. Her foot kicked something in the dark. She tripped and crashed forward. Arms flailing, she hurtled downward. She cried out and squeezed her eyes shut as her body hit the stairs. Her limbs tumbled over one another, twisting and hitting against the edges of the steps. When the rolling stopped, Charlotte was aware of Nell shouting her name just before she passed out.

Half an hour later, with great embarrassment, Charlotte had been helped back up the stairs. Mrs. Thomas's candle had revealed that there was no one hiding in the dank hole of a basement. Charlotte's left ankle was sprained, and she leaned heavily on Nell's arm when they left.

She couldn't walk to Haworth with a sprain, but a few blocks away, Charlotte flagged down a neighbor who delivered wool from the home wool combers in Haworth to the Armley Mills. He agreed to pick them up on his way back and take them home.

Back at the parsonage, after concocting a tale about stepping in a pothole and twisting her ankle, Charlotte borrowed an old cane of her father's. That night, she wrapped her ankle heavily in strips of cloth to make the swelling go down so she wouldn't need a cane the next day. Vanity or not, she had no desire to look crippled.

After everyone retired to bed that night and Charlotte was alone with Nell, she brought out her publisher's letter. "My editor looked for information on Edward Smithwick as well. He lied too. He's not an agent for a fire and life insurance company. In fact, Smithwick has a real motive for killing Mary—revenge."

She handed the letter to Nell, who moved closer to the fire to see clearly. Her voice was soft as she read aloud. "It's possible that Smithwick was in Leeds to see Mr. Green. I thought Edward Smithwick's name sounded familiar. I went to the London *Times* to search their newspaper archives. He went to jail last year for thirty days for threatening the banker. Mr. Smithwick vowed revenge for Mr. Green foreclosing on his London store."

Nell handed the letter back, and Charlotte refolded it. "It wouldn't have been difficult for Smithwick to discover that the banker doted on his only daughter."

Nell frowned. "But killing someone in revenge for a foreclosure sounds very unlikely."

"We don't know that that's all Mr. Green did to him," Charlotte said. "But it's a place to start."

Up in Charlotte's bedroom, they laid their plans for going to London. There was no fire in the cold grate, and Charlotte opened the bedroom window to let in some breeze blowing across the moors. Long after Nell was breathing deeply in sleep, Charlotte lay awake, contemplating various strategies as her ankle throbbed. The plans that had sounded so brave and sensible in daylight felt reckless and foolhardy in the dark.

What in the world am I doing? She wasn't the police.

But, she remembered grimly, the police thought Anne was a thief. And that cold, sneering Inspector Tipp had promised he would call on them soon. She had to have some solid answers before that.

13

Sofia's hands shook after her close escape. Thank heavens for Pat Cooper. She must have seen Sofia head toward the science room and realized the trap she was in. Sofia glanced in her rear-view mirror on the way out of the school parking lot.

"Do we have to go to Goodwill?" Wynter complained. "People might think we shop there."

"So what? You don't have to go in," Vanessa said. "Keep your whiny self in the car."

"Girls, please. It won't take long, Wynter. Stay in the car and do homework, if you want."

Vanessa had a list of items she needed for scenery, and she had a purchase order signed by the play's director. Inside the store, she marched off in search of decorative items and some old clothes. Sofia was glad to let her go. She needed a calming breather.

"Hello, Mrs. Parker."

She turned around to find Adam Jeffries and his grandfather. "Are you getting things for the play too?" Sofia asked.

"No." Mr. Jeffries held up a plastic bag. "I donate Adam's clothes here. Every time I turn around, he's grown two more inches and has outgrown everything."

"I understand," Sofia said. "I have the same problem with Matthew and Luke."

He patted the bag. "Goodwill always welcomes used jeans and athletic shoes."

"Not ours." Sofia shook her head. "By the time Matthew wears Luke's hand-me-downs, not even Goodwill would want them."

Adam decided to help Vanessa hunt for what she needed, and in a short time, she'd found everything. Ten minutes later, they were leaving the store and crossing the parking lot when a group of boys emerged from the Mini Mart grocery next door. Looking toward the Suburban, Sofia noticed Wynter slide down in her seat, out of sight.

What Sofia heard stopped her cold.

"Hey, Vanessa! Do you shop at Goodwill now that your dad got fired?"

Vanessa hugged her sack of items closer. "Wanna make something of it?" she called back.

Sofia cringed. She could tell by the rigid set of Vanessa's shoulders that she wasn't as untouched as she made an effort to sound.

The Jeffrieses were parked next to the Suburban. "I'm sorry," Mr. Jeffries said in a low voice. "So callous." He opened his car door, and several books and a large manila envelope slid to the pavement.

Sofia stooped down to help pick them up.

"Thank you," he said. "I'd better get to the post office before it closes." He tapped on the Suburban's back window. "See you tomorrow, Wynter!"

Sofia waved at him, climbed into her vehicle, and wearily headed home. The moment she had five minutes to herself, she'd call Officer Quimby for an update. They all needed some encouraging news. She got her chance while she cooked supper, but she almost wished she hadn't called.

"We're still pursuing leads," the officer said, "but there's nothing definite yet."

Yorkshire, England
July 1848

Charlotte and Nell were up before dawn to catch the earliest train for London, partly to be able to return before dark. Even more importantly, Charlotte wanted to avoid her father's concerns about railroad crime, which could escalate to an order to stay home. It was easier to sidestep his lecture and leave a note on the dining room table before setting off. With her ankle wrapped securely, Charlotte barely limped. Her parasol could double as a cane if necessary.

The train ride was uneventful, but the Euston Station in London was a marked contrast to the sleepy Keighley Station where they'd boarded. The classic architecture was beautiful, but Charlotte found the noise overwhelming. Passengers streamed off the train on Platform 1, jostled by other passengers, and picked their way through the milling crowd of friends waiting to greet arrivals.

On Platform 2, a train was ready to depart. Dozens of people had come to send off their friends or family members. Porters rushed everywhere, moving luggage on their trolleys, and Charlotte had to dodge several to avoid being run over. The noise of a locomotive letting off steam rose above the tumult.

Outside the station, there weren't many cabs to choose from. While Charlotte preferred a two-wheeled hansom cab, the only one available was a four-wheeled growler with its luggage carrier. In less than twenty minutes, they were deposited at the address of Mr. Smithwick's tiny, first-floor flat. The building was the color of dusty bricks. Two painted pots sat on the top step, each holding a plant that long ago had shriveled in the heat. One pot also held the burned ends of cigars.

Charlotte limped slightly up the steps to his door, where she knocked sharply with her curved parasol handle. There was no sound from within, even after she knocked again.

"Now what?" Nell asked from the sidewalk.

Charlotte stepped off the tiny porch and moved to the single window that overlooked the street. A small gap where the flimsy, water-stained curtains didn't come together offered her a miniscule view of Mr. Smithwick's sitting room. While she couldn't make out many details in the gloomy room, it looked terribly cluttered, more like a storage room than a home. Ceramic figurines of at least a dozen birds perched on the mantel and the windowsill.

Charlotte scanned the street, which was oddly deserted at this hour. Her glance lit on the pub at the corner, the Hare and Hounds. "Come on," she said, setting off. "There's the man in the neighborhood who will know the most."

Nell was horrified. "You can't go into a public house."

"I must." Charlotte tried to ignore the rapid hammering of her heart. "You can wait here."

Nell shook her head. "You can't go in alone." She took Charlotte's arm. "I'll come with you."

The pub was dark and nearly empty at that hour of the morning, although a few customers had already drifted in. Standing behind the counter was the landlord, a tubby man of medium height with a bald head offset by a drooping walrus mustache.

"What can I get you ladies?" he asked.

"Some information, I hope," Charlotte said, her nose wrinkling at the overpowering smell of stale spirits. "Where might I find Mr. Smithwick? He's not at home."

The landlord eyed her, then Nell, without comment. Then, apparently deciding that they meant no harm, he gave Charlotte a different address. "It's where his grocery business used to be. He was foreclosed on. He and his wife used to live in the flat above his shop. Ned often visits the empty shop and stands outside, reliving the past."

"And his wife?" Nell asked.

"Dead. Died during the bank business."

Charlotte frowned. "I understand he had his Bank of England loan through a bank branch in Leeds. Would that be right?"

"Aye. No London bank would renew his loan. Said his shop was no longer competitive."

After getting the address of his former home and directions for walking the six blocks, Charlotte and Nell set out to find the commercial area. The first block was so quiet it felt deserted, but the next two-block stretch they passed through was filled with drab tenements offering lodgings to families with armies of children. The streets were alive with them, playing, arguing, threatening, and fighting. Stray cats and dogs abounded, sniffing around Charlotte's skirt.

They passed out of that area before reaching a commercial area where Mr. Smithwick's grocery had once been a thriving family business. The shop now stood empty. Shutters covered the plate-glass window in front, but the small pane of glass in the door permitted Charlotte and Nell to peer inside the shadowy shop.

"A sad sight," Nell murmured.

Charlotte nodded. The shop's display cases, which had once held fresh fruits, vegetables, coffee, and spices, were empty, as were an overturned barrel and several crates. Racks behind the counter that had once been filled with merchandise were empty.

"Now what?" Nell asked.

Charlotte shook her head. "I wish I knew."

Charlotte turned and searched the street, but she couldn't spot Mr. Smithwick anywhere, nor did she see a pub on this block of stores. Next door was a tobacco store; she could smell the cigars through the open door. She paused by its smudged window, staring without really seeing the assortment of pipes on display.

Suddenly, a portly man with black hair liberally streaked with gray appeared in the open doorway. "Can I help you ladies?" he asked eagerly. "Are you shopping for a husband or a brother?"

"I'm sorry, but no." Charlotte turned to walk away, but then paused. "Have you been in business long?"

"Ten years." He waved a plump, hairy hand toward his window. "As you see—"

"Then you must know Mr. Smithwick," Charlotte said. "Mr. Edward Smithwick?"

"Ned? Of course. A good shopkeeper."

"I met him some time ago," Charlotte improvised, "and I thought he lived here. I was given this address."

"I'm afraid you wasted your time. He went out of business." The tobacconist rubbed the heavy stubble on his face. "Corner shops like Ned's couldn't compete anymore. Shoppers know about department stores now, and they want many goods under the same roof, not just food. Ned didn't change, and he lost customers." The man shrugged. "He couldn't pay his loan, so they foreclosed on him."

"How sad," Charlotte said, hoping to keep him talking. "I understand that his wife died as well."

The shopkeeper hesitated but then responded. "After they lost the shop, they were told to move out of the flat up there." He gestured to windows overhead. "Ned blamed her death on the bank. Said she died from worry."

Charlotte glanced meaningfully at Nell. His banker had been Mr. Green in Leeds. Had Ned Smithwick sought an eye-for-an-eye revenge for his wife's death by killing Mary Green?

Looking up, she noticed movement reflected in the shop window, someone watching them from the alley across the street. Charlotte whirled around and shaded her eyes against the sun's glare, but the alley entrance was empty.

Charlotte felt she had learned as much as she could there, so she thanked the shopkeeper, who flagged down a hansom cab to take them back to the bustling Euston Station.

It was even more hectic than it had been two hours before. Standing on Platform 2 after buying their tickets, Charlotte was jostled first one way, then another.

"I can't wait to board the train and sit down," she said. Despite the heavy wrapping, her ankle had swollen.

"How is your pain?" Nell asked.

"Worse, but our train should pull in any moment."

Charlotte bent over to check the bandage on her ankle. As she stood up, she was knocked off-balance. She stepped backward, beating the air to regain her footing. Instead, she pitched forward and fell down onto the tracks. She jerked her head to the side before landing but came down hard on her left arm. Pain shot from her elbow through her shoulder.

Stunned, Charlotte lay on the rails below the platform. And then she heard it: the whoosh of steam as a train curved around the bend.

"Charlotte!" Nell screamed on the platform above her. "Somebody help her!"

Charlotte kicked at her tangled skirts. The train's brakes were applied, producing a fireworks display of sparks. Its wheels skidded and shrieked along the rails as it barreled headlong toward her.

14

Cabot Falls, Vermont
Present Day

*H*anging up after talking to Officer Quimby, Sofia noticed a scrawled message by the phone in Jim's handwriting. *Rosa called. Call her back.*

Her heart sank, remembering her last conversation with Rosa and her promise to target Italian names. Calling her back would have to wait until after supper, when the kids were in bed and she'd planned out her candy class for the next day.

By bedtime, she was nearly out of time, but she'd put off the call as long as she could. Grabbing her notebook and the leather quilt diary, Sofia dialed her sister.

"Sorry so late," Sofia said and then explained about her evening.

"No problem," Rosa said. "I know how busy you are, and I'm sorry I put more pressure on you the other day. I didn't mean to, but I expect that's how it sounded."

Sofia let out a sigh of relief. Her big sister hadn't called to interrogate her about the quilt; she'd called to apologize.

"Don't worry about it. I'm nearly done teaching the special home ec classes, and then I can get back to the quilt research."

"That's what I wanted to tell you," Rose said briskly. "I shouldn't have pressured you. I should have helped you instead, so that's what I've done."

Sofia couldn't help it. Her spirits plummeted. "Help me how?"

she asked, making her voice sound as pleased as possible.

"I've been doing some research myself in the rare books collection at the university since we talked." She paused, and Sofia half expected a drum roll. "I think I've found that connection we talked about with Carlotta, Mario, and Gianni."

Sofia sighed, but she hadn't meant for her sister to hear it.

"Don't worry," Rosa said, laughing. "I know it's late. In fact, I just called earlier to tell you that I photocopied the research and mailed it to you today." She paused. "I realize I haven't been any help really, so I wanted to do this for you."

Sofia glanced at her notebook, where she'd made notations from her research. "My friend Marla works at the library here and has been a big help too."

"I'm sure she has been, but she's not family," Rosa said firmly. "And let's face it, the books at the Cabot Falls Public Library can't possibly compare to the Cornell University collection."

Put in my place again, Sofia thought wryly. But she couldn't argue with that.

Sofia stayed on the couch after hanging up and went over her notes again. Was she as wrong as Rosa seemed to believe about the possible origin of the lavender paisley silk square? They'd researched through the Brontë Society in the United States and England, plus a genealogy website and message board.

She'd also read quite a bit in the biography by Charlotte's friend Elizabeth Gaskell. After Brontë's death, her friend Ellen Nussey had written to Charlotte's family in 1855, asking them to commission a biography that would challenge the speculations in the press made about Charlotte and her sisters. Accusers had suggested that the author of *Jane Eyre* had forfeited the right to keep the company of respectable women because of her vehemence and passionate writing.

Sofia felt real empathy for Charlotte, who was falsely

accused of misconduct. Even more, she identified with the loyal friend, Ellen Nussey, who demanded to have Charlotte's name cleared. That was exactly how she felt about Jim. And like Ellen with Charlotte, Sofia's loyalty had to translate into action on Jim's behalf. She was determined to clear his good name, despite the school administration being content to condemn him.

Yorkshire, England
July 1848

"Help her!" Nell Nussey screamed again.

Charlotte regained her senses, tried to stand, and fell back on the tracks. Above her, Nell was on her hands and knees, leaning down to Charlotte. But her fingers were still at least five feet above her.

The screeching grew closer while sparks flew and spectators screamed. Then a guard jumped down on the tracks, scooped Charlotte roughly into his arms, and threw himself backward against the lower edge of the platform.

Charlotte closed her eyes against the suffocating steam as the train screeched past, not stopping for another twenty feet. Gritting her teeth against the throbbing pain in her shoulder, she thanked the Lord and the guard for saving her.

Her rescuer apologized for being rough, then handed her up to another guard standing above. Nell hovered over Charlotte. "Are you all right?" she asked, trotting alongside the guard who carried Charlotte to the waiting room for ladies.

"Ma'am, rest here while I get the stationmaster to fetch a doctor," the guard said.

She held her arm close to her side. "I don't need a doctor."

"Yes you do," Nell said firmly, shooing the guard on his way. "Whatever happened?"

"I bent over to check my sore ankle and—"

"Did you faint?"

"No." Cradling her arm against her, Charlotte stood to peer out the streaky glass of the waiting room. "I was pushed."

"It's these crowds," Nell said. "People are aggressive, trying to get the best carriage seats."

"No, Nell," Charlotte said, turning from the window. "I mean I was truly pushed, and not by accident. I felt someone's hand firmly on my back. I tried to move, and the pressure on my back increased. I was shoved off the platform."

The color drained from Nell's face, leaving her complexion nearly as pale as her light-blond hair. "Did you see who it was?"

"No, the person was behind me. After I hit the ground, I only remember seeing the train coming at me!"

Just then, a mother and her three young daughters joined them in the waiting room. The mother stared with some alarm at Charlotte's disheveled appearance. Within minutes, the stationmaster arrived with help. "Miss? This good doctor was in the gentlemen's waiting room. He's agreed to check your injuries."

"It's just my arm, and it feels better already." Charlotte straightened it gingerly, then bent it again. "Nothing is broken."

The physician examined her arm anyway, recommending that Nell tie a shawl into a sling until they got home. "It will make the bouncing train ride more comfortable." He stood. "Next time, stand back from the edge of the platform. You're very small and easy to bump."

But I was pushed! Charlotte wanted to scream, but she had no wish to terrify the little girls watching her closely.

"Accidents do happen." The stationmaster's tone was kind. "You're a lucky woman. You could have been killed."

Charlotte nodded and said nothing until he left, followed by the mother and young daughters. "Yes, I could have been killed. Someone *wanted* me dead."

"But who?" Nell asked, adjusting her shawl into a makeshift sling.

"I don't know." Charlotte looked up suddenly. "I saw someone, Nell! When we were talking to the tobacco shopkeeper, I saw a man in the reflection of his store window. He was standing across the street in the alley."

"Can you describe him?"

Charlotte sighed. "No. It was the briefest glimpse, just enough to know it was a man. When I turned around, he'd disappeared." She gripped Nell's arm with her free hand. "He must have followed us to the station and waited for his chance."

Nell glanced nervously at the door. "Who do you think it was?"

"Edward Smithwick. Maybe the pub owner repeated the questions I asked about him. He could have followed us to his old shop." She took a shuddering breath. "He knows I wouldn't be asking about him if I didn't suspect him of killing Mary."

"Then you must tell that inspector about this."

"I should," Charlotte agreed, but she knew she wouldn't. Not yet, anyway. He had practically ordered her to stay in Haworth, and she had no intention of doing that.

The nearly four-hour ride back to Keighley was painful for the first half of the trip, but Charlotte's arm and ankle felt somewhat better by the time they arrived. Keeping the arm in a sling helped, and during the part of the trip that they had the carriage to themselves, she elevated her sore ankle. At Leeds, Nell alighted to buy her tea and a scone from a vendor, but Charlotte stayed on the train and out of sight. She had no desire to run into Inspector Tipp, if he was still around.

When they arrived at Keighley, Charlotte used her parasol as a crutch.

"Are you sure you can walk?" Nell asked.

"Yes, my ankle is better," Charlotte said. "Before leaving town, I want to stop at Armley Mills one more time. James Thomas might be there now. I want to confront him about the lies I *know* he told."

"If you're sure," Nell said doubtfully.

Within fifteen minutes, they were climbing the stairs to the supervisor's office. Mr. Broderick stood at his window, chewing on his unlit cigar as he watched machine wool combers below. "Yes?" he snapped.

"I'm still looking for James Thomas. Is he here today?"

"You missed him." Mr. Broderick waved his stubby cigar through the air. "He up and quit this morning! He's worked for Armley Mills for nigh on twenty years, since he was a lad."

"Did he explain why?"

"No." He pointed at the machine workers below with the soggy end of his cigar. "The bloke he works with said he was behaving strange."

"How so?"

"Running up debts. Buying nice clothes for himself. Now, I ask you, what's a wool comber need with a top hat?"

Charlotte frowned. "What do *you* think he is up to?"

"I wager he will disappear and leave the debt behind."

"His wife told us that his mum died and left an inheritance."

Mr. Broderick raised a bushy eyebrow. "News to me."

Charlotte thanked him for his time, then took a direct route this time to the Thomas home. Mrs. Thomas was outside with two of the children. "Is your husband home yet?" she asked.

"He's in Liverpool," the youngest boy piped up.

His mother kicked open the front door and shoved him inside.

"Is that true, Mrs. Thomas?" Charlotte asked.

"What if it is?"

"Did you know he quit his job today?"

A stunned expression flitted over her face. "Of course I knew," Mrs. Thomas said defiantly. "He's gone to Liverpool." She wouldn't meet Charlotte's eyes. "He inherited his mum's house. As soon as it's his, free and clear, we'll all live there."

Charlotte couldn't decide if Mrs. Thomas was lying to her or lying to herself. "Do you have a street address in Liverpool?"

"Of course I do!" She spit out an address on Gorsebank Road.

"I wish you all the best," Charlotte said, moving off down the road.

"Do you believe her?" Nell whispered.

"I believe that's what her husband told her, but I'm not even sure she believes his story. The timing is too coincidental. James Thomas has money for new clothes, claiming it's from an inheritance from a conveniently deceased mother. It just *happens* to coincide with thefts from railroad passengers. I doubt Mary was the first. Had he stolen jewelry before and pawned it?"

"What is your plan now?"

"Hobble home, unless someone gives us a ride along the way." Charlotte sighed. "Then, after a good night's sleep in my own bed, we go to Liverpool."

Despite Patrick Brontë's vigorous objections, Charlotte and Nell were on the train to Liverpool early the next morning. It was only two hours from Keighley, and when they arrived, the Liverpool cab driver found the address with no problem.

It was a very modest home, but larger than the Thomases' flat in Keighley. Charlotte had barely withdrawn her hand from knocking when the peeling front door flew open.

"Yes?" It was James Thomas, although he wasn't as dapper as he'd been that day on the train.

"Mr. Thomas, I was among those questioned the day Mary Green died."

He frowned, then his expression cleared. "What do you want?"

"Some answers," Charlotte said boldly, glad that her long skirts and petticoats hid her trembling legs. "I know you lied about living on Canal Road. And you've worked for Armley Mills for nearly twenty years as a wool comber. You don't sell medical instruments." She shifted her weight off her sore ankle.

His eyes flashed, and his lip curled. When he finally spoke, his quietly controlled voice was full of fury. "Get out of here. I don't have to answer your questions."

"No, you don't have to," Charlotte agreed. She raised her voice when she saw a curtain twitch next door. "But Inspector Tipp will want to know how a man with a wife and four children can afford to quit his job. Where's the money coming from?"

Nostrils flaring, James Thomas noticed a neighbor leaning out his window. Thomas moved back. "You'd better come inside."

He closed the door behind them, and Nell stayed close to Charlotte. The cluttered parlor, with its fading wallpaper, sparse furniture, colorless paintings, and threadbare carpet, seemed the ideal home for a widow. It was a place to withdraw from life surrounded only by what was worn and familiar.

"My life is none of your business," he said, gritting his teeth.

"The police have accused my sister of a crime you may have committed, so it *is* my business," Charlotte said.

"My mum died last week. I buried her yesterday." James Thomas pointed to two photographs on the mantel, one of his family and another of himself with a very wrinkled elderly woman. "I grew up in this house, and I inherited it as oldest son."

Nell cleared her throat. "Excuse me, but these furnishings do not look like the home of someone with extra cash tucked away. We understand that you've been buying new clothes lately. Where did that money come from?"

"There was a little money from my mum." He stepped closer and raised a hand threateningly. "I don't care if you believe me or not. Now get out of my house."

Charlotte and Nell left quickly and didn't speak until they were a block away. Charlotte stopped to catch her breath, leaning heavily on the handle of her parasol. Across the street, a young beggar stood with his cap out. He hurried toward them, smiling as he said some garbled words.

Nell reached into her reticule for a shilling. The boy took it, grinned, and moved away. "So sad to see the deaf begging like that," she said.

"One of the people on the train when Mary died was a schoolmaster on holiday from Doncaster, one of those schools for the deaf."

Nell took Charlotte's arm as they moved on down the street. "I only wish those schools could teach them a trade so they didn't end up begging. My poor nephew at the Manchester deaf school isn't learning anything useful."

"At Doncaster they do," Charlotte said. "Mr. Hopkins talked about them learning to make shoes and going on field trips to museums. He said they have a good life and jobs after they leave."

"Really?" Nell asked. "Manchester is considered the best deaf school in the north. My brother and his wife made sure of that before sending Arthur there." She was quiet for a moment. "I could be wrong, but I think my brother said Doncaster closed last April after a major outbreak of tuberculosis. He was so glad Arthur wasn't there. I don't think the school has reopened yet."

Charlotte mulled over her friend's words. Had she overlooked something obvious, just because she had liked the schoolmaster, George Hopkins? Was he really not on a school holiday? And Nell said the deaf schools didn't have the results he claimed.

If Nell was right, why had the teacher lied?

15

Cabot Falls, Vermont
Present Day

At breakfast the next morning, Sofia was still stinging from Rosa's phone call as she served scrambled eggs and biscuits and tried not to trip over Fergus, who circled her legs. As she urged the girls to eat more, she realized she had a couple of expert test takers of her own to interview. And with Jim gone, taking Luke to school early for a robotics club meeting, he couldn't tell Sofia again to please stay out of it.

"Let me pick your brains a minute," she said, sitting across from Wynter and Vanessa.

Matthew snickered. "Not much to pick there."

Wynter rolled her eyes. "What would you know about brains?" she asked, salting her eggs.

"A lot more than you!" He grabbed two biscuits. "What does a brain do when it sees a friend across the street? It gives a brain wave."

Wynter rolled her eyes again, and Vanessa groaned.

Matthew grinned. "When does a brain get afraid?"

When no one paid any attention to him, Sofia asked, "When?"

"When it loses its nerve."

Sofia grinned. She could always count on Matthew for comic relief. "Eat your breakfast." She turned back to the girls. "I wanted to ask you something about the monitoring system at school when you take tests."

"No system." Wynter shrugged. "The teachers stand like hawks at the front and give you the evil eye if you look like you might talk," she said. "And they make you put your phones away so you can't look anything up."

"I thought they used webcams to watch students," Sofia said. "That's what I heard anyway."

Vanessa smeared butter and dripped honey over her biscuit. "I had to take a big test once with kids from another class. We did it in the auditorium, where they have webcams mounted up high. They didn't tell us we were being watched, but I saw the red light go on and the camera move slowly back and forth. I know from theater productions that as long as that little red light is blinking, it's recording. No one would dare to fool around or cheat, even if the teacher stepped out."

Sofia thought for a moment. "Could a student or someone stop the webcam somehow? Or could someone else stop it from a computer in another room maybe?"

"Using spyware, you mean?" Wynter asked.

"I don't know about spyware, but could they?"

"I doubt it," Vanessa said. "If someone could stop the webcam, students would pull out notes or use a cheat copy of the test to get answers."

Sofia nodded but thought, *What if?* If a wireless webcam could be started up again from a remote location, would anyone even notice a missing piece in the middle of the video? Did anyone actually go back and watch the videos later?

"Finish up and brush your teeth," Sofia said. "I need to get my makeup on, and then we'll go."

But minutes later, as she stared at her eyes in the bathroom mirror, Sofia lost focus and her hand stopped moving. That computer lab teacher, Michael Daley, still seemed like the key. He would know about starting and stopping webcams, wouldn't he?

And students took makeup tests after school in the lab sometimes. The publishing center was right next door, and lots of the tests were printed off there. Couldn't Mr. Daley somehow copy the tests to sell later to students?

It sounded possible. But how could she possibly prove it?

Yorkshire, England
July 1848

The next morning, although Charlotte and Nell were up very early, Patrick Brontë was waiting for them in the sitting room when they brought in their breakfast bread and tea.

"Oh, you're up!" Charlotte set the pot of tea on the dining table. "I'm sorry if we awakened you."

He nodded solemnly. "We need to speak."

"Certainly, Papa." Charlotte handed Nell a thick slice of bread and kept one for herself. "But we don't have much time before we catch the 6:24 to Leeds."

"You are putting yourselves in danger!" her father protested. "Why must you go to Leeds?"

Charlotte chose her words carefully. Her father still didn't know that Anne was suspected of stealing Mary Green's jewelry and therefore tangled up in her murder. "Anne and I are witnesses and will have to testify at the inquest soon. I want to ask the inspector when it will be." She added milk to her tea. "I also want to find out the results of the autopsy. It was surely performed days ago."

"Autopsy!" Mr. Brontë spluttered.

"Of course, Father. They do autopsies whenever there is a suspicious death."

"I know that," he snapped. "I am appalled that *you* know about such gruesome things as autopsies and inquests. These are no subjects for ladies."

Charlotte laid her hand gently on her father's sleeve. "Papa, I would infinitely prefer staying home, walking the moors with Nell, writing stories, enjoying the quiet country life." She sat as tall as she could. "But I won't be a prisoner in my own home, just to suit the inspector." *And I won't let him back Anne into a corner so he can arrest her.*

Charlotte took a big bite of bread and butter, thankful that their servant, old Tabby, had baked yesterday. She would pack sandwiches for their trip today too.

Muttering under his breath, Patrick Brontë stalked across the hall and disappeared into his study, closing the door with more force than was necessary. Charlotte sighed and followed Nell back to the kitchen to pack a wicker basket with food. "I hate that Papa thinks my behavior is inappropriate for a lady. Soon, he'll be agreeing with all my critics in the press."

Nell gripped Charlotte by the shoulders, bent down, and looked her eye to eye. "If Mr. Brontë knew why you were so actively hunting Mary's attacker, he would be astounded and applaud your courage."

"I hope he never has to know," Charlotte admitted. "Nor Anne. She grows ever more frail."

"I know I'm not any real help to you," Nell said, "but if there is anything I can do, you must let me."

Tears filled Charlotte's eyes, and she blinked them back. "Not letting me be alone in my pursuits is the best thing you can do."

By the time they reached Leeds, Charlotte had formulated a plan. She would brave Inspector Tipp's wrath and demand to know the autopsy results. If she was right—if Mary had been drugged before being robbed—it should prove Anne had nothing to do with it.

But when they entered the stationmaster's office, they learned that Inspector Tipp no longer used that room as his temporary office. "He's moved to a railroad police box just a mile down the line to the south."

Charlotte sighed and glanced at Nell. Hiking up the rail line for a mile was not what she'd expected, but it made sense that the inspector would move there. It must be one of the bigger octagonal ones.

"Thank you," Charlotte said, glad she had tightly wrapped her sore ankle. "It's a nice morning for a walk."

"No need for that," the stationmaster replied to Charlotte, but he smiled at Nell. He stepped outside the office, searched the platform, and strode over to a police constable. After a short conversation, the officer nodded, set off to the south, and the stationmaster returned. "Constable Healey will let the inspector know of your arrival. Would you like to wait here? I could get you tea."

Charlotte hid a smile. She had no illusions that this gallant behavior was on her account. She had always been small and plain, but Nell—the focus of Woodford's smiles—was a genteel, well-dressed, very attractive lady.

"We don't want to bother you," Nell said. "Perhaps you could inform the inspector, when he arrives, that we will be in the ladies' waiting room."

"Certainly."

Outside, Charlotte whispered, "You disappointed him."

Nell gave a delicate *humph*. "I would rather pay for my own tea."

But after more than an hour passed, Charlotte wondered if the inspector was even coming. "Maybe the constable returned with a message," she said. "Maybe the inspector wants me to walk to his station. Or he has refused to see me. Neither would surprise me."

They returned to the stationmaster's office. Charlotte was amazed by how much hotter the day had grown after just an hour in the cool waiting room.

The stationmaster was still alone in his office. He glanced up, obviously pleased, when they arrived.

"No inspector yet?" Charlotte asked, standing in the doorway.

"No, but the constable returned some time ago and said Inspector Tipp would be here shortly."

Charlotte hoped so. He'd made it clear during their last encounter that he thought she was interfering and ignorant about police work. *Maybe I am*, Charlotte admitted to herself, *but Inspector Tipp is just as ignorant about my sister.*

"I don't think he's coming," she finally said. "He probably plans to delay so long that I'll give up and go home." She nodded her thanks to the stationmaster. "The inspector doesn't know me very well. If he won't come here, I will walk to his station."

"No need," came the clipped voice behind her.

Charlotte whirled around. Inspector Tipp nodded and lifted his stovepipe hat. Today, he was again immaculately attired in a frock coat and striped trousers, although his trouser cuffs were coated with dust from his walk. Charlotte had read that the respectable clothing was to reassure the public that allowing a police force some power was not the beginning of military rule. They dressed like honorable gentlemen instead. For her part, Charlotte was glad she didn't have to do their laundry.

Charlotte and Nell moved farther into the stationmaster's office, and Inspector Tipp followed them in and closed the door. "Now. How may I help you ladies?"

Charlotte bristled. Although his tone of voice was respectful in the extreme, she felt he was looking down his beak of a nose at her. Perhaps it was his air of extreme patience, as if he were dealing with a dotty old aunt.

"I came to ask about Mary Green's autopsy," she said with no preamble.

"What about it?"

"I want to know if the doctor found that I was right."

A wary expression replaced his aloof detachment. "Right about what?"

"That Mary was given laudanum to knock her out before she was robbed. Did the doctor find more laudanum in her body than what was in her medicine dosage? Is that how she was murdered?"

The inspector pulled out his pocket watch, glanced at the time, and clicked his tongue in irritation. "I know you are an authoress, Miss Brontë," he said, "but we deal in facts, not stories you concoct to cover up your . . . involvement."

Charlotte wanted to scream, but she glanced at Nell and read the warning in her eyes. She clamped down on her temper instead. Swallowing hard, she lowered her pitch to sound as refined as Nell. People always listened when Nell spoke.

"It's true that I make up stories, Inspector Tipp, but that doesn't mean I live in a fantasy world. We receive many newspapers in Haworth, and I keep up with world events." She turned to the stationmaster. "Mr. Woodford, would you agree with me that you have seen an increase of crime on your trains? That thieves are more audacious, yet cunning, and they do more planning?"

The stationmaster looked from Inspector Tipp to the ladies. He clearly didn't care to antagonize the inspector, but as Charlotte had hoped, his desire to impress Nell won out. "Yes, the thieves are crafty and getting away with more. I'm sure Inspector Tipp would agree."

The inspector said nothing, but his nostrils flared.

The stationmaster cleared his throat. "As an example, last year, we caught two thieves—brothers, they were—who were stealing from goods trains. Their work called for planning and, as you say, Miss Brontë, audacity." He moved to a map of the rail lines nailed on his wall. "One brother chose stretches of the line where freight was slowed down by an incline or slope, like here and here." He stood tall, his chest puffed out and hands on hips. "Armed with a pile of sacks, the younger brother would leap into an open wagon of a moving train, stuff items into a sack, and throw it out on the grass. He was agile enough to move from wagon to wagon, stealing things that would not break when thrown and which were easy to sell."

"And the older brother?" Nell asked. "What did he do?"

"It was simple, really. His job was to follow the train with a cart and pick up the bags of stolen goods. Since they only took small amounts from the total cargo, the thefts went unnoticed for a time."

Charlotte could hardly contain her excitement. "I saw something thrown from the train before we pulled into Leeds that day!" She went to the map. "It was just before a tunnel under a stone bridge. Near that spot." She turned back to the inspector, but he remained silent. Her patience ran out. "Don't you see? There was a thief on the train that day, maybe part of a team. If only the constable had gone to look when I reported it."

"Miss Brontë, I'm a busy man," Inspector Tipp said. "Let me do my job. You go home and do yours. I meant what I said. Stay out of the investigation." He tipped his hat at the ladies, then left the stationmaster's office and strode off down the platform.

Charlotte wanted to stamp her foot in frustration and anger. "Let's go, Nell," she said. "Mr. Woodford, thank you for your help." With a curtsy, the two ladies left.

"I will go buy our tickets back to Keighley," Nell said.

"No, not yet," Charlotte said. "Why didn't the inspector answer my question about the autopsy? What is he hiding?" She retied her bonnet strings. "Inspector Tipp is lying about something."

"Not necessarily. I imagine that being evasive with civilians is part of his job."

"Oh Nell, you are too nice. Well, if he won't tell me anything, there's more than one way to skin a cat." She passed by the ticket counter and under the overhanging roof. On the street side of the train station, Charlotte got her bearings, then pointed. "He's that way, on Neville Street."

"Who is?"

"Dr. Thornton. I expect the Greens' family doctor either did the autopsy or knows who did. I must know what medical evidence he plans to give at the inquest. I won't be blindsided by whatever the inspector is hiding."

The doctor's office was only four blocks up Neville Street. Nell offered her arm, but Charlotte shook her head and leaned on her parasol.

Soon, they stepped into the doctor's empty reception area. It had a ten-foot ceiling, was paneled halfway, and was plastered above that to match the ceiling. Immense landscape paintings hung from decorative hooks. Three tall windows behind the doctor's massive desk had small, beveled panes of glass.

Charlotte was about to call out when a woman entered from the back of the office. "Hello! I'm Mrs. Thornton. My husband is out on a call and not likely to be back for hours."

Charlotte let out a frustrated sigh. "May I leave a message for him?"

"Of course."

Taking out pencil and paper, Charlotte wrote quickly. Before she finished, she became aware of footsteps somewhere in the office, behind a door that perhaps led to the family rooms. Was the doctor really gone? Or like the inspector, was he refusing to talk to her?

Charlotte skirted around the doctor's wife, strode to the closed door, and opened it. Coming down a staircase was Dr. Thornton. He stopped halfway when he spotted her.

"So you're here after all," Charlotte said, glaring back at the doctor's wife.

He licked his lips. "What can I do for you?"

"I have urgent reasons to know what you discovered when you performed Mary Green's autopsy. I am trying to clear my innocent sister's name."

"I'm afraid that I can't help you."

"Did you do the postmortem?"

"I can't help you. I'm sorry."

"Did another doctor do the autopsy then?"

"No . . . uh, I . . . did not do an autopsy. I can't tell you any more."

Charlotte was fed up with hearing that. She retied her bonnet with a jerk. "Fine. I'll go to the Greens' home and tell them to demand an autopsy. It should have been done days ago."

She headed to the door, but the doctor ran down the remaining steps and grabbed her arm. "Wait. Don't do that."

"Then will you help me? What are you all hiding?"

The silence in the office was thick and tense, almost alive. Dr. Thornton clenched his hands into tight fists at his sides. "I did not do an autopsy because they are only done on the deceased." He closed his eyes briefly. "And Mary Green isn't dead."

16

On Thursday morning during one of her candy-making classes, Sofia received a message from Pat Cooper saying she needed a ride home after school that day. Sofia sighed. She was so tired by the end of the day, and Pat could talk nonstop.

Then she scolded herself. *Pat is in this because of me.* Yes, she was tutoring, and she was undoubtedly helping students, but her sole purpose for being at the school was to help the Parker family.

Sofia made an attitude adjustment, signed the note *Happy to give you a ride!,* and sent it back.

So at three thirty, Sofia put on a smile, put some energy in her step, and sailed into the library. The last few days, they'd been using Pat in the publishing section, a small room off the main library. Her face lit up when Sofia arrived.

"Come here and see this!" She moved over so Sofia could see a website. "It's called FotoForensics.com. It has tutorials that allow you to determine how much a photo has been edited, using what is called an error level analysis."

Sofia studied the screen and frowned. "I don't understand."

"Remember how we thought maybe the tests weren't stolen because someone could have taken a photo of them instead?"

Sofia nodded, still puzzled.

Pat stepped behind Sofia and closed the door to the small room. "What if someone is paid to raise a student's grades by fixing a paper or test? You take a photo of a paper the student has done, change some of the answers—for a price—and then print it out again, all corrected. Instant grade improvement. Then, in case someone questions how a student got an A when the grade book says a C, the student has the A paper to show. *Voilà!* It looks like the teacher got it wrong." She grinned. "But run that new paper through the error level analysis, and it just might tell you what changes were made."

"Yes, I can see how that might happen," Sofia said. "I'll study the website later at home. Thank you for showing it to me." She opened the door and motioned for Pat to follow. "Wynter's waiting at the car, and I need to pick the boys up at their school now."

"Sure. Of course." Pat grabbed her bag and followed Sofia through the library.

Out in the hallway, students swarmed around the lockers, and Sofia felt like she was a salmon swimming upstream. Pausing to let a group get past her, she spotted Mr. Jeffries. They all walked out together.

"How's your day been?" Pat asked him.

"Very rewarding," he said, "but my old brain is tired. I just spent two hours helping a young man analyze three scenes in *Hamlet*."

Pat's face lit up. "Shakespeare! That's wonderful. Lucky boy to have your help."

"He'd been absent for several days, so there were homework assignments and a quiz," Mr. Jeffries said. "We made good progress. My brain is ready to rest though!"

Out in the parking lot, Sofia walked ahead of them, past Mr. Jeffries's older-model car on the way to her Suburban. Sofia wondered briefly why Mr. Jeffries's car engine was making those crackling, cooling-off noises. The car must have arrived only minutes ago. She started to say something but then realized what must have happened. Adam must have taken the car and run a quick errand after school. Mr. Jeffries probably knew about it.

And if not, Sofia thought, *I'm not going to blow the whistle on his grandson and cause that nice older man to worry.* She had enough troubles of her own to worry about.

Yorkshire, England
July 1848

Charlotte stared at the doctor, openmouthed. "Not dead?" she asked, shaking her head in disbelief. "Mary Green isn't dead? Why would you lie about something like that?"

Dr. Thornton took three strides across the room to his desk and sat down heavily. "I didn't lie. Not intentionally anyway. I really believed she was dead."

"How could that happen?" Charlotte demanded.

"She had all the signs pointing to death," the doctor said. "When I arrived at her train carriage, she was cold already. She had no detectable heartbeat, no breath I could discern, and no other signs of life. She was even becoming stiff." He shook his head as if even he couldn't believe it. "I didn't have to think twice about declaring her dead."

"When did you realize your mistake?" Nell asked.

"After we moved Miss Green to her home to be readied for a wake and her funeral." His tone was pleading. "You have to understand. Her physician in London had given her medicine with laudanum in it. Mary wasn't—isn't—a very big woman. She might have taken too much medicine by accident. She went into a heavy coma, which sometimes mimics death very well."

Charlotte gritted her teeth. "And Inspector Tipp knows what happened?"

"Of course. I reported it immediately and have been attending Mary since."

"Then why the secrecy?" Charlotte demanded. "Inspector Tipp refused to answer my questions about the autopsy when he knew there hadn't been one—and why."

"I can't help you there," the doctor said, spreading his hands wide on his desk.

Head still spinning, Charlotte pounded down the packed dirt road, barely noticing the impact on her sore ankle, and made it back to the train station in half the time.

"Slow down a bit, can you?" Nell asked, her breath coming in short gasps.

"I'm sorry." Charlotte slackened her pace. "You sit and wait here at the station. I'm going to the police box down the tracks to confront Inspector Tipp."

Nell grabbed her arm. "You won't have to." She pointed to the vendor near the end of the first platform, where the inspector was paying.

Charlotte nearly ran down the platform, calling, "Inspector Tipp! I've just been to Dr. Thornton's office and—"

He dropped his sweet roll and grabbed her arm in one swift motion. "Keep your voice down!"

"Let go of me." She jerked loose. "How dare you keep the news from me—"

"Stop." He glared at her from beneath the brim of his top hat. "Keep the volume down, or I'll take you into custody for interfering in a police investigation."

Her sides heaving, Charlotte prayed that she wouldn't faint from the tightness of her stays. With Nell following, she let herself be half walked, half dragged back to the stationmaster's empty office. Inside, Inspector Tipp closed the door firmly and directed Charlotte and Nell to two empty chairs.

"So it's true that Mary is alive?" Charlotte asked.

"Yes," he said grimly. "But unless you can manage to keep quiet, you'll sabotage the investigation. She was robbed, and there was an attempted murder, we believe."

"I want to see her. She's at home, the doctor said." If Charlotte had known about this, she could have returned the letters she'd taken for safekeeping. Mary no doubt had panicked when she realized they were missing.

"I forbid you to go there. Do not call attention to the house. We don't know yet if it is being watched."

"Why didn't you tell me about Mary earlier?"

"Because you didn't need to know. The investigation is bigger than just Mary Green. And if you refuse to stay out of it, I'll take you into custody and get you out of circulation myself." He scowled again at Charlotte. "We are looking for a career criminal, a thief who's been active on the train line for months and is getting bolder. If we don't publicly correct the doctor's mistake—if we let this criminal assume Mary is dead and can't testify against him—he will feel safe, thinking he can't be identified. The thief will get cockier and make a fatal mistake."

Charlotte admitted grudgingly that it made sense. "So is my sister no longer a suspect?"

"Until we arrest someone else, she is still a suspect." He leaned closer, his hook nose reminding Charlotte of a vulture's beak. "You seem to forget one very important fact: your sister was found with some of the stolen jewelry on her, which you hid and then lied about. She is still our most likely jewel thief."

Charlotte shivered involuntarily. Anne's health wouldn't hold up during a trial, and she wouldn't last a month in a prison.

"All right," Charlotte admitted. "Yes, we hid the cameo brooch after Anne found it in her reticule. We panicked and lied. But what about the lies of the others who had access to Mary Green's carriage? Did you check all their statements?"

Inspector Tipp rolled his eyes. "Please don't tell me how to do my job, Miss Brontë."

"Somebody has to!"

Nell gasped, but Charlotte ignored her. "Did you know, Inspector Tipp, that Mr. Smithwick had his loan foreclosed on by Mary Green's father? and that his wife died soon afterward? He hated Mr. Green and even publicly threatened him and went to jail for it. And what about James Thomas? He lied about his job, where he lived, and why he was in London. We don't think that the Doncaster schoolmaster was all he claimed to be either."

"Are you quite finished?" The inspector's tone was icy. "I know about Mr. Thomas and his basically harmless attempts to impress Celia May. Mr. Smithwick's loan was foreclosed on over a year ago. We kept an eye on him after he went to jail for threatening Mr. Green. He's been calm since he adjusted to his wife's passing. And the schoolmaster was on holiday because his school was closed due to a widespread illness." He paused. "So you see, Miss Brontë, I've not been sitting and waiting for you to do my job for me." He marched to the office door, his boot heels hitting the floor hard. "Now go home. And *stay* home."

Charlotte gathered up her things, leaning more heavily on her parasol. She stepped outside, heading toward the ticket window where she and Nell would part company. Charlotte would miss Nell's support.

"By the way," Inspector Tipp called after her.

With great reluctance, Charlotte turned and faced him.

"Tell your sister that I will be over to see her." He paused. "Very soon."

His face was pleasant and he even almost smiled, but Charlotte felt the threat behind his words as much as if he'd shaken a fist at her.

17

Cabot Falls, Vermont
Present Day

Thursday evening after supper, while the kids worked on homework, Sofia got out her own. The home ec teacher wanted Sofia to quiz the students the next day on what they'd learned. She didn't plan to make the test hard at all, just have them sketch a personal design they'd like to try on a cake and define some cooking terms.

While Jim had started working with the boys on their math, Sofia had gladly slipped off to the living room. She was partway into Elizabeth Gaskell's 1857 *The Life of Charlotte Brontë*. She'd just spotted something exciting when the doorbell chimed.

Fergus barked as he raced from the dining room to the front door and back, yipping in his high-pitched tone. He scratched at the front door. "Stop that," Sofia said. "Settle down."

Sofia grinned when she found Marla on her doorstep. "Come in," she said, opening the door and holding the dog's collar. "I was just going to text you with something neat."

"Hi, Jim. Hi, kids." Marla waved as she followed Sofia to the couch. She patted the leather shoulder bag. "I've got something exciting for you too." She sat down and said, "You go first while I catch my breath."

"I discovered that Elizabeth Gaskell, who wrote Charlotte's biography, spent time in Italy. I can't find that Charlotte ever traveled there, but it's a thread to follow that will make Rosa happy. And it's a way that Charlotte's piece of clothing could have traveled there even after Charlotte's death."

Marla was practically bouncing on the couch. She opened her shoulder bag and removed a manila folder full of papers. "I found out the same thing, and guess what? Do you know *where* in Italy Gaskell traveled?"

"No, not yet."

"She went to a city by the name of Bronte. It's in Sicily, on the west side of the volcano Etna."

Sofia felt as if her heart had stopped beating. "There's a city named Bronte in Italy? Really?"

"Yes, it's a rural area famous for its pistachio nuts."

Sofia laughed, but it was followed quickly by a frown. "It might tell me how the silk shawl got to Italy, but it doesn't tell me who my ancestor is. Charlotte never made it to Italy."

"I can't answer that, but we've got a start." Marla handed over the folder of papers. "I couldn't take the books out of the library research room, but I made photocopies." She stared closely at the pages and patted her wavy blond hair. "Sorry. Looks like I accidentally shed a hair on the photocopy machine."

"That doesn't matter!" Sofia laughed and patted Fergus, who kept putting his nose into her lap. "I deal with shedding hair all the time."

After all the kids were in bed, Sofia read the photocopied information from Marla more slowly. Her excitement built. It should be enough to satisfy her sister for the time being, enough to show Rosa that Sofia's gut instincts could well be on target.

She had started putting the papers away when she noticed again the photocopied information on Bronte in Sicily, the page with the wiggly black line caused by one of Marla's hairs. That line was proof it was a copy. Sofia stood perfectly still, trying to grasp the idea flitting around at the back of her mind.

Copies, not originals. Spotting doctored documents. FotoForensics. Error level analysis.

She had another gut feeling, that these ideas flitting around in her head fit together somehow, some way, in the grade-fixing scheme at the high school.

But how?

"You coming to bed soon?" Jim said, stopping on his way back from the kitchen with a banana.

"Yes. Now, actually."

Forcing a smile, Sofia gave up on her tired brain and decided to sleep on it. She hoped that by morning, some of the pieces would fall into place.

Yorkshire, England,
July 1848

The knocker sounded during breakfast the next morning. Charlotte wiped her lips and hurried to the door. Anyone calling at this time undoubtedly had an emergency, but her father had left an hour earlier to console a parishioner's family whose nine-year-old son had succumbed to scarlet fever.

Charlotte swung open the door and froze. Inspector Tipp

stood on the step, his teeth glinting below his hawk-like beak. "Miss Brontë, good morning."

Stunned and speechless, Charlotte stepped back. The inspector removed his top hat and followed her across the wide entrance hall into the dining room, where her sisters were finishing their breakfast. While she'd told her family that Mary was alive, she'd minimized the inspector's continuing suspicions. The mild curiosity in Emily's eyes contrasted markedly with the stark terror in Anne's. Charlotte nearly choked on her words when she introduced Emily to Inspector Tipp.

"Excuse me for interrupting your meal," Inspector Tipp said smoothly, not sounding sorry at all. "My visit won't take long."

He surveyed the sparsely furnished room slowly and methodically. On one wall was an engraving, a picture of the queen. On each side of the high, narrow, old-fashioned mantelpiece were two recesses filled with books. Charlotte realized the decorations were scant. The plain furnishings showed that the Brontës lived simply and frugally.

But to the inspector, she feared, it only proved what he already suspected: that money from three spinsters' writing wasn't enough to keep body and soul together. *Not unless we supplement our income by pawning stolen jewelry*, she thought.

Charlotte swallowed the sour taste in her mouth. "How may we help you, Inspector?"

He answered her but studied Anne. "We must examine each person's opportunity and alibi," he said. "Your sister had the cameo brooch in her reticule and was seen leaning over the victim." He cleared his throat. "A few inquiries at the Black Bull in the village led me to believe that you ladies have easy access to laudanum, the drug used to render Miss Green unconscious."

Charlotte felt the blood drain from her face, but she said nothing. She could hear Emily's agitated breathing, but from Anne, not a sound.

"Your brother?" Inspector Tipp prompted.

"Our brother, Branwell, is quite ill in bed," Charlotte said stiffly. "He has such medicine for his seizures."

Emily stood up so quickly that her chair crashed over backward. "I'm going to get Papa."

"No!" Anne's protest was barely above a squeak. "I don't want to upset him with this."

"You're right," the inspector said. "I won't be here long." He reached inside his frock coat, removed a folded piece of paper, and laid it on the table. "I have a search warrant here for Anne Brontë's bedroom."

Anne gasped. Charlotte grabbed the paper. "You can't just show up with a search warrant!" Charlotte cried. "Right to privacy is a law now. Search warrants were made illegal more than fifty years ago."

"Those were general warrants, Miss Brontë, where we could come in anytime and search without a specific goal and take anything we wanted." The inspector's patient tone of voice annoyed Charlotte. "My search warrant today shows where I can search and what I can look for—specifically, the missing jewelry and Mary Green's other stolen items."

"This isn't right," Charlotte argued. But she read the wording on the search warrant with a sinking heart. It appeared to be legal.

He turned to Anne and gave a quick, stiff bow. "Please show me to your room."

Anne turned paler, if possible, at the idea of this policeman pawing through her things in her private bedchamber. But Charlotte saw no way around it, not with this warrant. Besides, she wanted the inspector gone before her father returned.

"I'll escort him upstairs," Charlotte said grimly. "Emily, stay with Anne."

Still fuming, Charlotte climbed the wooden staircase, passed the ticking grandfather clock on the landing by the window, turned, and ascended to the top floor. She crossed the upper hall to Anne's bedchamber and pointed inside.

"You needn't stay," the inspector said. "I shan't be long."

"I'll stay." Charlotte hoped her glare conveyed the massive distrust she felt for this man. Apparently, it did.

Inspector Tipp rolled his eyes. "I don't intend to plant something to incriminate your sister," he said with a sharper edge.

She made no response but watched his every movement as if he were a noxious bug under a microscope. He searched under her bed, in all her bureau drawers, under chair cushions, and beneath the two small rugs beside her bed. On hands and knees, he examined the seams in the hardwood floors, apparently looking for secret compartments beneath the floorboards.

While he replaced drawers and clothing, Charlotte remained planted in the doorway. "Well, Inspector? You didn't find anything, did you?"

"I didn't honestly expect to find anything here. Would she really hide stolen goods in her own room? More likely they're buried in the flour bin or out on the moors or in the graveyard next door. Unfortunately, my warrant doesn't cover that."

Charlotte stepped closer to him and lowered her voice, afraid that Branwell across the hall might hear her. "Why aren't you looking more closely at past railway crimes? You said you were looking for a career criminal."

Inspector Tipp smiled, but it was more like a sneer. "Yes, I *am* looking for one—or possibly two—thieves who have been sly enough to ride the rails and steal small amounts and not be suspected." He leaned close. "Like two plainly dressed spinsters maybe?"

Charlotte gasped. She had never wanted to slap someone so badly in her life. She clenched her fists where she hid them in the folds of her skirt.

The inspector studied her closely. "Who would suspect them? Jewelry stashed in reticules or, as you mentioned, a thief could throw a bag or reticule out the train window just before coming into a station. It would be a simple matter to walk back along the track and pick up their loot . . . perhaps on their walk home to Haworth." He bowed. "You'll be hearing from me again, Miss Brontë."

Furious and frightened in equal measure, Charlotte followed him down the stairs and through the hallway. She jerked the front door open and wished she had the nerve to push him forcefully down the front steps. Instead, her father was coming up the walk.

Nearly choking on her words, Charlotte introduced her father to the inspector.

"An inspector?" Patrick asked, frowning. "Why are you here?"

"Your daughters are helping me with my inquiries."

Charlotte wanted to argue. She wasn't helping him. She was trying to help her sister. But her father didn't know that Anne was a suspect, so she bit her tongue.

Patrick shook his head. "I'm sure you can find the lawbreaker without bothering my daughters. Please don't come again."

The inspector bowed and headed off down the cobblestone street. They watched him till he was past the graveyard, around the corner of the church, and out of sight.

"Well, that's that," Patrick Brontë said. "He understood me, and he won't be back."

Oh, Papa, Charlotte thought, *if only you're right*. But she knew in her heart that she'd cross paths with Inspector Tipp again, and before long.

After finishing her breakfast, Charlotte was too agitated to settle down and work on her newest manuscript. She finally threw down her pen. "I need a walk on the moors."

Emily glanced up from her writing desk. "Do you require company?"

"No, I wouldn't be good company for anyone." Besides, Charlotte wanted to think, to sort out what she knew from what she suspected and figure out her next step for protecting her sister. Downplaying the seriousness of Anne's involvement with her family had worked until this morning, but now what?

At the last minute, she grabbed her father's old cane to use for a walking stick in case her ankle began to hurt. For the next two hours, she walked, at first so deep in thought that she barely noticed her surroundings. She was alone most of the time, seeing only two shepherds with their flocks of sheep. She passed a cluster of crumbling stone outbuildings and an old stone farmhouse. The back door of the farmhouse stood open, but Charlotte passed by.

By noon, the July heat was unbearable, and wispy clouds overhead promised no rain for some hours. After resting by the stream near a waterfall, Charlotte picked her way around peat bogs and headed back down the hills to the parsonage. Everywhere she stepped there were little streams and bogs and wet rocks to slip and slide on. The downward path was easy to follow, but the hillside was so steep that she had to walk down sideways to keep from sliding. She was exhausted when she reached Haworth, but her spirits had settled some.

Charlotte forced herself to write that afternoon, but there was no joy in it for her. She wanted Anne to think she wasn't worried, that the inspector's visit had been nothing but a formality to cross them off his list.

But she knew differently.

By bedtime that night, the little breeze had died. The hour-long soaking rain during the evening hadn't cooled the air. Charlotte tried to enjoy the July heat. It was the only month on the mountainous moors that they truly had summer weather. She pushed her bedroom window up as high as it would go, kicked her father's old cane back under the bed, and blew out her candle.

She lay awake for what seemed like hours, tossing one way, then another. The gibbous moon provided enough light for her to make out objects in her bedchamber: the candleholder, a rocking chair, the polished bedposts, the limp curtains at the window.

Charlotte had no idea how long it took her to fall asleep, but sometime in the night, a sharp sound awakened her. She was curled on her side, facing the wall, and she assumed the sound had come from outside. She often heard footsteps on the cobblestones as men found their way home late at night from the pub.

But then she heard it again, only much closer. She could barely breathe, and when she did, it was too shallow to ease the sudden pain in her chest. Her mind raced crazily, yet her limbs were frozen. Ever so carefully, ever so slowly, Charlotte rolled over on her back. Out of the corner of her eye, in the shadows of her bedchamber, she spotted a movement.

Someone was in her room.

A dark-coated figure stood by her wardrobe. He was big and burly, like a brown bear, with a ragged cap pulled low on his forehead. Had he climbed up the heavy grapevine on the trellis outside her window? Or had Papa forgotten to latch the doors at bedtime again?

His boots sounded on the wooden floor when he moved to the carved box where she kept her correspondence and a bit of money. "No!" she cried and threw back her quilt.

The intruder whirled around, his shape clear against the moonlight coming in the open window. From his bulky outline, Charlotte immediately thought of Edward Smithwick.

She opened her mouth to scream.

He bounded across the room in two steps, grabbed Charlotte's pillow, and forced it down on her face. Charlotte thrashed and kicked, pushing and clawing at the pillow, but the pressure only increased. Arms flailing, she tried to do damage to the man's head and face, but she kept grabbing his coat instead. He wasn't nearly as heavy as she'd thought. Inside the bulky coat was a thinner person, someone much too slim for Smithwick. Charlotte felt herself begin to lose consciousness. Dizzy and faint, she lost strength. Her fingernails caught the intruder's hand or wrist, and Charlotte dug in. When he shook her off, she knew she had his blood under her nails.

Before she could roll sideways, he'd pushed the pillow back on her face. Stars flashed behind Charlotte's eyelids.

"Stop!"

The pressure on her face suddenly released, and Charlotte pushed the pillow off. She drew a ragged breath, and then another, the stars clearing. Charlotte finally realized that what looked like a ghost was Emily in her nightdress. She'd grabbed at the intruder, and Charlotte heard a rip. Charlotte gasped for breath, unable to move for a moment, and watched the nightmarish scene before her.

She had to help Emily. But how?

Charlotte remembered her father's cane and groped where she'd thrown it under her bed. Gripping it, Charlotte stood, braced her bare feet in a wide stance, and brought the cane down on the man's head. His cry of pain was followed by one of anger, and he reached for the stick. Charlotte struck more blows with the cane on his arm and wrist.

As she raised the cane again, he grabbed it and wrenched it from her, shoving her hard, so that she crashed into Emily. They both fell down hard. Charlotte rolled over in time to see the intruder drop the cane, climb out on her windowsill, balance a moment as he reached for the grapevines, and then disappear.

Charlotte heard the thud as he jumped to the ground below. She reached the window in time to see him disappear, weaving and stumbling, through the shadows in the graveyard.

Emily joined her at the window, clutching the cane. Charlotte hugged her trembling sister close.

"Who do you think it was?" Emily asked, a tremor in her voice.

"I have no idea." She closed her window, deciding she'd rather bake in the steamy night than be attacked again.

They went down together to double-check the front and back doors. Charlotte was grateful the family had slept through the incident, but she could hardly believe it. How was it possible that Papa was still snoring as they passed his bedroom door? She knew the parsonage's thick walls helped keep out the winter winds that whistled down off the moors, but she had not realized that so many other sounds were also blocked.

Upstairs again, Emily hugged Charlotte. "Are you all right?"

"Yes, thanks to your rescue." She gripped Emily's slender hand, then forced a smile and let her go.

But Charlotte stayed at the window, staring down the street to the church until she heard the clock on the landing strike 2:00 a.m. She could still hardly believe what had happened. Why? And why now?

Had the inspector told someone about searching their house for the jewels? He'd only had a search warrant for Anne's room, but someone had wanted Charlotte's room searched too. And then a thought struck her so hard she thought she might faint. Could it have been Inspector Tipp who came back to search what his warrant wouldn't cover? The man she had grabbed had been slim under the baggy coat, like the inspector. If only she'd been able to see his face.

She rolled her eyes at her own imaginings. As much as she disliked Inspector Tipp, she didn't believe he'd attacked her. No, that man played it by the book. But by the time she fell asleep, she was no closer to finding a solution.

In the morning, by mutual agreement, Charlotte and Emily

kept the events of the night from their father and Anne. However, long before he was up for breakfast, Charlotte had checked the rain-soaked flower bed beneath her window. Just as she'd expected, there were two clear prints in the mud where the intruder had let go of the grapevine and jumped the remaining five feet to the ground. She followed his footprints across the courtyard, the prints growing farther apart and deeper around the toes as he had picked up speed.

Back in her room, Charlotte dressed and straightened her coverlet. Turning, she spotted a piece of paper half under her chest of drawers. She picked it up and unfolded it. In a handwriting she didn't recognize, block letters said *KEEP YOUR GUARD UP.* Where had that come from?

She replayed the terrifying scene from the night before and recalled hearing a rip after Emily had tackled the intruder. She had grabbed at the man and must have torn a pocket in his pants or jacket—a pocket that held this message. What in the world could it mean?

Charlotte tucked it into her reticule. When she spoke to the inspector later, it was the *second* thing she planned to show him. At long last, she had solid evidence.

Thankful that it was no longer rainy, Charlotte found the bag of powdered plaster of Paris where Tabby kept it in the kitchen. They occasionally used it on wet bandages to make a stiff support for a sprain or cracked bone. Other times, they plastered over stains caused by leaks in the ceiling. But that morning, Charlotte mixed wet plaster for something entirely different.

She carried the bowl of soupy paste outside and carefully poured some in each impression the intruder had left in her flower bed. It wouldn't take long to harden, and then she'd remove the solid impressions for a permanent record.

But later that day, when she delivered the note and a plaster mold of the intruder's boots, Inspector Tipp was not impressed. "Half the men in your village have this kind of boot. It's a common size and a common sole." His eyes grew hard as bullets. "Go home, Miss Brontë. Stick to the kind of storytelling your publisher wants."

Charlotte wanted to cry in frustration, but she bit down hard on her lip. He thought she'd written the note herself and made up the story about the intruder! He probably thought she'd made the molds using Papa's or Branwell's boots.

Well, she'd go home all right. She'd even ask the local watchmen to walk by the parsonage more at night. But she wouldn't spend her days writing more stories. No, not until she'd solved the real horror story that had become their lives.

18

Cabot Falls, Vermont
Present Day

Although Sofia was pleased to be teaching her last classes on Friday, she felt an element of panic as well. She'd been at the high school for two weeks, but what had she really accomplished for Jim? According to their lawyer, he and the science teacher were still the main suspects in the cheating scandal.

"Scapegoats, you mean," Jim had muttered darkly.

Because she was only giving the home ec students a simple quiz for her last day, Sofia had a full hour free during the lunch period. She found Pat and asked her out for lunch. "Well, out in the car, anyway," she said. "I packed some sandwiches, and we need to talk. This is my last day here, but will you continue? How can I help if I can't be inside the school?"

Over chicken sandwiches, apple slices, and candies made by the home ec students, they pooled what they knew—and what they suspected.

"Let's write everything down, no matter how silly it sounds," Pat said. "I'm a great believer in lists. I'll talk, and you write."

Sofia first listed what they'd overheard at the athletic field and also what they suspected. "You know the cheaters will only approach rich kids, many of them jocks, who have money but poor grades and want athletic scholarships," Pat said.

"Yes, or their parents want them to get into good schools, and they need top grades for that." Sofia sat back, leaning her head against the headrest. "But how did someone get a test of Jim's? The test wasn't missing, and his laptop wasn't messed with."

"Don't forget, though, about the fake call to get him out of the classroom."

"And the intruder who attacked him that Sunday night." Sofia shuddered. Being knocked down by the person in the dark hoodie and black high-top shoes had left an indelible memory.

"I still think someone, probably that student, scanned and photographed the test with his or her phone." Pat snapped her fingers. "Kids are experts with their phones nowadays. They could print the test from the photos and then sell it."

"True, but if overseeing tests, like with webcams, is part of the mix, doesn't that mean another teacher is involved, not just a student?"

"You mean a teacher and student working together?" Pat asked.

But Sofia didn't answer. Instead, she stared out over the parking lot, forgetting the rest of her lunch as something nagged again at the back of her mind. What was it?

Then, without even trying to make sense of it all, things began to fall into place in her mind, almost like a slot machine, where each image of a peach or a cherry dropped into its place. One. Two. Three.

And the way things lined up made her almost sick to her stomach.

One. Adam Jeffries knew how to operate webcams from his work videotaping the play. Did his retired grandpa have enough money to supply his needs, let alone his wants? Had that been Adam Jeffries in the stairwell, dressed in a dark hoodie and high-tops? Sofia drew in a sharp breath. And was that why they were really at Goodwill? Had Adam outgrown the jeans and shoes, or did his grandfather need to get rid of them because they might be recognized and tie him to the break-in?

Two. One day after school, Mr. Jeffries had claimed he'd been working with a student on Shakespeare makeup assignments for hours, but when they'd gone out to the parking lot, Mr. Jeffries's car engine was still cooling down. Someone was lying. What if he'd only been at the school a few minutes, just long enough to meet with the student, turn over homework Mr. Jeffries had completed himself, and collect the fee he charged for his "service"?

Three. At the Goodwill store, when things had fallen out of Mr. Jeffries's car, Sofia had picked up two books and a large manila envelope, a lumpy envelope that Mr. Jeffries said he needed to mail. But now, as clear as day, she remembered something that her mind had barely registered at the time. That envelope had been addressed to Mr. Jeffries himself, at a post office box. Whatever he had mailed to himself for safekeeping—notes, tests, flash drives—could sit in a post office box for as long as he needed to keep it hidden.

"Listen to this quick," Sofia said, ticking off the three points on her fingers. "I have to get back to class now, but I'll contact Officer Quimby right after school." She gripped Pat's arm. "Keep your eyes sharp, but don't do anything. I mean it, Pat. If I'm right, Adam Jeffries injured Jim, and he won't mind hurting you—or me."

Yorkshire, England
July 1848

The two nights following the incident with the intruder, Charlotte slept little. And the night before, Branwell had cried out in his sleep too many times. Charlotte would give anything to calm the demons that terrorized him both day and night.

Sitting at her portable writing desk at the dining room table, she had only written half a sentence when her pen left a great blot of ink on her page. She was dabbing at her manuscript when the knocker on the front door banged once, then after a pause, again.

Wiping at her hand with an inky rag, Charlotte went to answer it. "Yes?"

On the doorstep stood a young woman, her black hair pulled back in a twisted braid. Her tiny glasses with tortoiseshell rims and yellow, smoked lenses didn't hide her bushy eyebrows. She glanced at Charlotte's inky hand and smiled broadly. "Are you Charlotte Brontë, authoress of *Jane Eyre*?" she asked eagerly.

Charlotte's greeting froze on her lips. Who was this young woman in her dark, severely cut outfit? It reminded Charlotte of a riding habit with its fitted jacket, long skirt, and mannish top hat.

The girl's smile faded, replaced with uncertainty. "I'm sorry," she said, the wrinkles in her forehead deepening. "Let me begin again." She shifted the schoolgirl satchel she had strapped diagonally across her body. "I'm Lucy Taylor, and a friend of mine from Manchester, Lenora Matthews, was on the train last week coming up from London, and she overheard a constable saying that Charlotte Brontë from the parsonage in Haworth was really the writer of *Jane Eyre*." She finally stopped to draw breath.

"I'm afraid I don't know your friend," Charlotte finally said, wondering how to get rid of the curious visitor. Was this to be her life from now on? Perfect strangers showing up on her doorstep to gawk at her?

"Lenora doesn't know you either, but we're both such great fans of your writing, and when she told me what she'd overheard, I said to her, 'Lenora, you can't be right! The author of our favorite book ever can't live but forty miles away!'"

"Thank you for your kind words," Charlotte said, reaching to close the door. "Now that you have seen me, you can tell your friend."

"Oh no, please wait! I didn't come to stare at you, but to ask you for some writing advice about how a woman like you can make it in a man's world and get published and write something with such power and passion." She laid a gloved hand at her neck. "I've read your reviews, many of them, and I said to Lenora, 'This is a woman like us who's an independent feminist, a brave woman, and not tied to a man either. I simply must meet her in person.'"

Charlotte felt assaulted by the avalanche of words, and yet there was something about this Lucy that appealed to her. Perhaps it was that she was so enthusiastic and yes, so naive, about writing and publishing. It reminded Charlotte of herself a long time ago.

"So you're a writer too?" she finally asked.

"Yes." She patted the satchel hanging from her shoulder. "I always have my manuscript with me."

Charlotte tried to hide her dismay at this piece of news. "That is very dedicated of you."

"Oh, no, don't worry," Lucy said. "I didn't bring it to make you read it, and I won't bother you with it or ask you to give me ideas or anything like that. No, that's not my intent at all. I just couldn't know that the authoress of *Jane Eyre* lived in Yorkshire and not ask you for some advice on breaking into the writing and publishing field because the writing life is my dream, and it's been my dream for longer than I can even remember, ever since early girlhood anyway, when my brother and I made up so many stories and plays and we invented games and even wrote little books." She gasped for air.

Charlotte grinned. That decided it. "Your childhood is a mirror image of mine with my brother and sisters." She swung the door open. "Do come in. I can at least give you some tea after your trip here." *But then I want you to go home*, she thought.

But after Lucy had passed another hour, in Emily and Anne's company as well, Charlotte was actually glad the young woman had come. Her enthusiasm and eagerness to learn any bits of writing wisdom they could share was both fun and flattering.

"What train home are you catching?" Anne asked Lucy. "If you have time, you should climb up on the moors and experience some of the places from Charlotte's book."

"I would love that!" Lucy said, smudging her eyeglasses as she pushed them back up to the bridge of her nose. "I don't actually have to travel home tonight because I reserved a room at Haworth Old Hall, but I haven't paid for it yet because I wanted to see first if it was even possible to speak to a writer so famous. But if you have even the smallest amount of time to talk to me today, I can stay over and catch the early train home tomorrow."

Charlotte could tell that her sisters liked Lucy, as she did herself, but they wouldn't answer for her or commit her to anything. She finally said, "I would be glad to talk to you about writing, and I wish I could ask you to stay with us." She pressed her lips together. "But our brother, Branwell, is very ill upstairs, and he often doesn't sleep well."

"Oh, no, please don't think that I was trying to wheedle an invitation out of you; not at all, no!" Lucy looked aghast. "Haworth Old Hall looks like a wonderful place to stay, and it was only a short walk up the hill from there, and I would be very honored to have an hour or two of your time because I know you have your own writing to do, and I don't want to take you away from that."

Charlotte felt herself grow breathless just listening to the young woman. Had Charlotte ever been that bubbling over with excitement? She wished more than believed it to be so.

Charlotte stood and gathered the tea things, loading the tray.

"Today, let's hike up to the moors. It's a beautiful day, and you can share your writing dreams with me." Charlotte decided to ask Tabby to pack some sandwiches to take along. "Then if you like, perhaps when we stop for a light picnic lunch, you can show me a few pages of your work."

"Really?" Lucy's eyes grew twice their normal size and were doubly magnified by her amber glasses. "Oh, Lenora will be so jealous, and she's going to wish she had taken off time from her job—she's a seamstress—and come with me!"

For two hours, Charlotte and Lucy climbed over the spongy purple moors and talked about writing. Taking long, manly strides, Lucy exclaimed over and over, at seemingly every turn, at scenery she recognized from Charlotte's book.

"Do you hike in the moors often?" Charlotte asked as they picked their way over sedgegrass and heather, choosing the peat-covered mounds for firm footing.

"No, I was born in Manchester and have lived there my whole life. What I know about the magical moors I learned from *Jane Eyre*."

"Well, you had better follow me then," Charlotte said, hopping from one mound to another. "These raised mushroom-shaped mounds are called peat hags. The drier, fluffier-looking areas of exposed peat can be counted on to hold your weight."

"What about that area?" Lucy asked, a bit out of breath from their steep climb.

"Those holes in the ground lead to underground streams and wetter sections," Charlotte said. "It's best to avoid them."

Lucy turned in a full circle and threw her arms wide. "So beautiful. So very, very beautiful!"

"Yes, right now it is wonderful up here, without the snow and icy winds. I wrote once that Haworth and these moors are a place where summer never comes." Charlotte knelt to spread a cloth in the heather for their lunch. "But people die on the moors too. For one thing, you will want to watch for adders in the grass." She laughed at Lucy's horrified expression. "And keep a watchful eye on the sky when on the moors. Storms blow up fast, often with hail, and you do not want to be caught up here then."

Now that Lucy's nervousness had worn off, or she'd calmed down, or perhaps was simply tired from the hiking, Charlotte found the boyish-looking girl a good companion. As they ate, Charlotte explained about the wild, steep valleys that split Yorkshire and Lancashire, where the wind howled over the moors.

"It can be lonely," Charlotte said, "and it is an increasingly lawless place. Sheep rustlers are around, although they're more widespread during the winter months when nights are longer. Sheep rustlers used to be hanged at Lancaster Castle, which is nearby." She unwrapped the cake she'd packed. "Because of rustlers, shepherds brave the cold blowing rain that is so common to keep a close eye on their flocks that huddle near all these drystone walls that snake over the hills."

After lunch, they passed several ruined stone dwellings plus two stone sheds. "There's a quarry nearby," Charlotte explained. Birds were plentiful too, making nests in the heather and the grass to lay their eggs and raise their chicks. Charlotte pointed out her favorite, curlews.

After hiking for two more hours, they were both grateful to head back down the hills. "I'll take you past one of my favorite spots, a waterfall that we built a bridge over. It's at its best after heavy rains. It can be a perfect torrent racing over the rocks, white and beautiful. But in dry weather, it is barely a trickle."

At the end of their hike, when they reached the graveyard outside the parsonage, Charlotte indicated one of the table grave markers for resting in the shade of the oak and ash trees. First, she read a few pages of Lucy's writing, which was remarkably fine for one so young. "You write with a depth one doesn't often see so early."

"You really think so? What advice can you give me to improve or to find someone who would publish me? Must I use a man's name to gain an audience with a publisher? Must I change my heroine and make her beautiful, as my friend Lenora insists? She reads my work, but she is not as impressed as you seem to be."

"Heroines do not have to be beautiful, no matter what others say. I once told my sisters that they were wrong—even morally wrong—to make their heroines beautiful as a matter of course. They swore that it was impossible to make a heroine interesting on any other terms. So I set out to prove them wrong. I showed them a heroine as plain and as small as myself, who could be as interesting as any of theirs."

"You mean Jane Eyre!"

They talked some more, until Charlotte realized she was very tired. "I have some domestic chores to do now, but I will leave you with this last bit of advice, perhaps the most important. One essential part of advice is knowing when to ignore it." She paused and grinned. "Three years ago, I wrote to the British poet Robert Southey to ask whether I should aspire to be a successful writer. His reply was cool. He told me, let me see, I want to quote him correctly . . . he said, 'Literature cannot be the business of a woman's life, and it ought not to be. The more she is engaged in her proper duties, the less leisure she will have for it, even as an accomplishment and recreation.' He also said if I got busier with a woman's duties, I would be less eager for celebrity."

Lucy laughed. "You didn't listen to him, did you? Nor did your sisters."

"No," she said, standing, "but sometimes those women's duties do call."

Lucy hesitated, then asked one more favor. "In the morning, I'll be catching an early train, but could we take one last hike up to the moors? I'll bring the food this time, some scones and fruit from the inn, and maybe see the waterfall one last time since it isn't far." She straightened her satchel, closed the buckle, and stood too. "If you can't, I understand. You have already been generous with your time. I am grateful you were my guide to this place where summer never comes."

Charlotte considered her words, then decided to go with her heart. "I'd love another quick walk in the morning. Today has done me much good, getting me away from . . ." She started to say "my troubles" but finished with a smile and said, "my domestic duties."

The next morning, Charlotte was awake well before dawn with a headache and dressed for the hike before anyone else was stirring. Branwell had kept them awake much of the night, and she hoped Papa and her sisters would sleep late. When they met outside the church, Lucy was bubbling over about her writing, and Charlotte enjoyed the brisk walk. They hiked to the waterfall almost without pause, and they passed an abandoned farm on the way back down.

"Wait!" Lucy said. "Did you hear that?"

"What?"

"An animal crying, I think, from that shed." Lucy headed across the peat, stepping carefully as Charlotte had told her. She opened the shed door and peered into the dark. "Something is back there in the corner."

Charlotte peered over Lucy's shoulder but couldn't see anything. "Where?" She stepped around Lucy and went inside, then waited for her eyes to adjust to the dim interior. She leaned closer but heard and saw nothing. "I think you were mistaken," she said.

"I don't think so." The shed door slammed shut, and everything went black.

19

Cabot Falls, Vermont
Present Day

As soon as Sofia dropped the kids off after school and picked Jim up, they headed directly to the police station. Using the same notes she'd written in the car while talking to Pat, Sofia laid out her suppositions and clues, one by one, that she felt pointed directly to Stephen Jeffries and his grandson, Adam.

Jim shook his head slowly. "Mr. Jeffries? The grandfather who's been so good to help Wynter?"

"I know," Sofia said. "I hate the idea too, but doesn't it make sense?"

Officer Quimby sat across from them at a table littered with empty coffee cups and half-eaten pizza. "I hate to think you're right," he said, "but it all fits together. The only thing is . . ."

Sofia's heart sunk. "What?"

Officer Quimby leaned forward and folded his hands on top of the table. "I expect you're probably right about the large envelope Mr. Jeffries mailed to himself. Unfortunately, I can't look into his post office box without a search warrant."

"How long will it take to get one?" Sofia asked.

"You don't understand. Even if I think your idea makes sense—and I do—it's not enough to get a search warrant to go through his mail."

"But he isn't going to tell you the truth if you ask him."

Officer Quimby thought a moment. "Let me check something."

He was gone five minutes, during which time Sofia and Jim held hands but said nothing. It was out of their control, and Sofia hated the feeling that she still hadn't done enough.

When the officer came back, he nodded. "It's like I thought. If you're right about how the grade fixing happened, I expect that much of the information—tests, answer keys, homework payments collected—is stored in the cloud somewhere. And when it comes to information stored there, a warrant isn't required. I'd need only a court order or a subpoena, which I can get easily enough. And if I find what I expect, then I can get a search warrant to open the post office box and examine that envelope."

"Should we come with you?" Jim asked. "Will you need me to identify copies of papers or tests that are mine?"

"No, not yet anyway. But after we round up the information—if Sofia is right about the culprits being the Jeffrieses—then I'll want you and other teachers affected to confirm that the stolen information is yours."

It was a long, restless evening at home. Sofia suspected that while the whole family watched an action movie together, neither she nor Jim was paying much attention to it. After Jim gave her a private lecture on the dangers of what she and Pat Cooper had been doing at school for two weeks, he gave Sofia a bear hug that left her breathless.

"I only hope we are right," she said.

Officer Quimby didn't call them Friday night nor all day Saturday. By Sunday night, Sofia had nearly given up hope when the doorbell rang. Fergus greeted the officer as if they were long-lost friends, and the police officer came inside to give them his update.

"It's good news and bad news," he said. "Which would you like first?"

Yorkshire, England
July 1848

Charlotte stumbled across the dark shed, tripping on the uneven ground, and fell against the door. Surely she wasn't locked inside! *Stop thinking like a panicky child*, she scolded herself.

She pushed against the door, but it was jammed somehow. The wind must have banged it shut. Or was it locked tight? Whatever the cause, she was caught in the shed on the moors. And all alone.

"Lucy?" Charlotte called. "The door is stuck." There was no answer. Nothing but the pounding of her own heart in her ears. "Lucy? Help me get out, please!"

Charlotte pressed her eye against the slim crack of light around the door and peered out. Her narrow view showed only the moorland grasses. She moved to the tiny gap of light on the other side of the door and saw nothing but a corner of the abandoned stone farmhouse.

"Lucy Taylor! Where are you? I'm trapped in the shed!"

What had happened out there? Had a marauding maniac attacked Lucy and locked Charlotte in the shed? Perhaps Lucy had been bitten by an adder or had wandered off to explore and sunk in a bog. Even as Charlotte's mind raced from one possibility to another, she knew she was grasping at straws.

Lucy hadn't been attacked or fallen into a peat bog. For some unfathomable reason, she had pushed Charlotte into the abandoned shed in the middle of nowhere and had slammed and barred the door. She was too far away from Haworth for anyone to hear if she screamed. Why had Lucy done this?

Charlotte faced the truth: She was trapped without food or water high up on the moor. How long would it be before someone found her? She rarely ran into hikers or shepherds in that area.

Charlotte gathered her skirts beneath her and sat down, back against the door, and forced herself to think and pray. She was unhurt, she'd already had breakfast, and before many hours passed, her sisters would look for her. It might take time to find this abandoned farm site, but they wouldn't stop searching until they found her.

Her heart slowly approached a normal rate of beating. First, Charlotte tried to figure out why Lucy would do this to her, but her mind bounced from one thing to another, and soon she gave up. It made no sense at all.

Think like you're going to write about this, she told herself firmly. Remember things. Reconstruct places, conversations, people . . . "I can use my time profitably while I wait," Charlotte encouraged herself. She rarely had uninterrupted time to think.

While keeping part of her senses trained for any sounds outside the shed, she got to work. If only she had her paper and pencils. Instead, she constructed a mental list of everyone who'd had contact with Mary the day she'd been robbed: Mrs. Green, Anne and herself, Smithwick, who stopped and spoke to Mrs. Green, Celia May, who joined their compartment at Sheffield, the guard, Nic, who talked to Mary while they rested on a bench . . . anyone else?

As hard as she tried to think methodically, her agitated mind bounced from one seemingly unrelated memory to another.

She recalled a guard's hat she'd found with a long hair in it. She remembered how Edward Smithwick and James Thomas had lied, but the truth she'd uncovered didn't prove them to be thieves. And there was George Hopkins. Nell doubted that he was a schoolmaster for the deaf, despite what he'd said.

But her mind always returned to Lucy. What had possessed that young writer to do such a thing to her? Or . . . *Oh no.* Charlotte shook her head slowly.

Was Lucy Taylor really a writer? The beautiful writing sample she'd shared had been so polished, so professional. Charlotte suddenly felt very foolish. Those pages had undoubtedly been copied from someone's published work, but she'd been so flattered by Lucy's gushing compliments that she'd overlooked the obvious. Remembering their initial meeting, but now knowing Lucy's plans for her, Charlotte scrutinized their time together with a critical eye.

If Lucy wasn't a writer, who was she? Why had she gone to such lengths to lure Charlotte away and trap her where she might not be found for days? *Who was Lucy Taylor?*

She tucked her skirts tighter around her shivering legs and pulled her shawl closer around her shoulders. And then it hit her. Charlotte's breath went out of her with a whoosh.

Of course. Underneath the outward appearance, the body and face shape and height were the same. Exchange the mannish clothes for a dainty dress, black hair for a blond wig, long, swinging strides for a mincy walk, boisterous talking for breathy flirting, and the transformation was complete. Lucy Taylor was Celia May!

Was the young woman an actress? Or was she only an expert at disguises?

Charlotte stood then, needing to walk, both to warm up and to think. With one hand touching the rough stone wall, she took tiny steps one way, paused, and then retraced her steps to the door. Back and forth, back and forth. Her racing mind grew calm as her feet paced.

Each time she was at the door, Charlotte peered outside through the narrow lines of light. Each time, there was no sign of Lucy. Could that slender Celia May possibly be the career criminal Inspector Tipp was searching for? Could she have perpetrated a series of railway thefts all alone? No jewelry was found on her—but she could have passed it to an accomplice if she had one. One who had tossed it out the window to pick up later. If so, who was her accomplice? Could it be the intruder who'd searched her room?

As she paced, Charlotte tried to gauge the time. It must be two hours since she was locked in. Lucy—or Celia—had long ago caught the train at Keighley. *Where are Emily and Anne?* Charlotte had stayed alert, but she knew no one had called her name all morning. If only she'd told someone that she'd planned to see Lucy again before she left! By now, even without that information, her family had to know something was terribly wrong.

But the day passed into the afternoon and evening. Charlotte noted through the gap by the door when the light changed direction and dimmed. Every half hour, or so she estimated, Charlotte pounded on the door with a chunk of wood she'd found in a corner. She pounded and screamed until her throat was raw.

No response.

Where were her sisters? Why hadn't they rounded up their friends and formed a search party? No one was left alone on the moors at night to face dangers impossible to see in the dark. While she was safe inside from peat bogs that could suck her under, she wondered if adders sought the warmth of abandoned buildings at night. They could certainly find the gap beneath the door.

Charlotte counted to a hundred, she sang songs and hymns, and she prayed. Even so, the image of snakes silently slithering toward her in the dark kept her awake and tense.

Saturday morning at daybreak found Charlotte stiff and cold, shivering despite her shawl wrapped tightly around her and her legs tucked under her skirts. She had finally slept toward morning. What woke her was the sound of thunder in the distance. She glanced up at the roof's pinpricks of light, trying to gauge the least leaky location in which to sit if the rain hit.

She tried the door again, hoping that the wind or some animal in the night had loosened whatever Lucy had used to bar it. But no luck.

Thunder grew louder, and Charlotte shook from cold and hunger and the beginnings of a migraine. Then, between thunderclaps, her ears picked up another sound. Was her mind playing tricks on her? She scrambled to the door, pressing first her ear and then her eye against the strip of light.

Yes! There was a barking dog and a deep voice calling to it. It must be a shepherd working his border collie. She opened her mouth to scream, then shut it abruptly. Should she yell for help or not? Did she hear a shepherd, or was he a sheep rustler? One would help her. The other wouldn't—and might kill her as well.

It took Charlotte only a few seconds to decide. She had to risk it. She screamed and pounded on the wooden door with the stick of wood. Within a minute, she heard the dog scratching at the door. Then there were footsteps and whatever was holding the door was knocked loose.

Charlotte pushed the door open and fell forward on her hands and knees. The barking dog circled her, pretended to nip at her, and then jumped back. One strong arm grabbed the border collie, and the other helped Charlotte to her feet.

After the shepherd gave her bread and water, Charlotte insisted on heading back to the parsonage. It was Saturday, and her father and sisters must be frantic. Weak and shivering, she stumbled over the moors.

She was halfway down the hills when she heard thunder again, behind her, yet closer. Within five minutes, cold rain was lashing at her back. Her heavy skirts and the bottom inches of her petticoats were soon soaked, and the sodden material tripped her. Stumbling and exhausted, she fell to the ground three times. Around her, the hillside disappeared into the growing gloom. Scudding clouds were low enough to make the day dark as evening.

Charlotte wiped the rain from her eyes and peered around. She knew where she was, or at least, she was almost sure. But stumbling about on the moors, especially during storms, was how people died.

She decided she couldn't go wrong if she kept traveling a downward path. She lost track of the passage of time, but she guessed it was another hour before she stumbled through the graveyard, into the garden, and staggered up the seven steps to the parsonage door. Once inside, she slammed the front door behind her and sank to the carpet.

Anne emerged from the dining room, pen in hand, and gasped. "Charlotte! What's happened to you?"

Her cries brought Emily and their father on the run. The astonishment on their faces was matched by Charlotte's hurt and shock. She'd been gone a day and a half, and her family was waiting out the storm in their cozy house, reading and writing!

Her sisters helped her into the dining room while their father ran for a blanket.

"What happened?" Anne repeated. "Is Nell with you?"

Nell? Charlotte tried to think. Why would Nell be with her? "I don't understand," she finally said, her voice raspy.

Emily reached across the table for a paper lying on Charlotte's writing desk. "We found this note when we got up yesterday." She laid the paper next to Charlotte.

It was the short note she'd received a week ago from Nell Nussey. *I'm eager to see you on Friday. Early train is 6:44.* At the bottom of the note was Charlotte's own scrawl. *Leave early Friday.* She remembered writing the reminder to herself to leave early in order to meet Nell's train in Keighley.

"I'm confused," Charlotte finally said, rubbing her temples. "Where did you find this?"

It was Emily's turn to look bewildered. "Where you left it for us on the dining room table yesterday. We saw it when we came in here for breakfast."

Anne nodded. "You were gone already, but we recognized Nell's handwriting. She obviously wanted to see you yesterday. Was it an emergency? We didn't really expect you back so soon."

As Charlotte warmed up, with two blankets around her and hot tea inside her, the migraine lessened so she could think. Gradually, the days' events began to make sense. "This letter from Nell was when she was *arriving* on her trip here. It wasn't a note asking me to come to her. This letter was kept in my desk in my bedchamber."

Papa stopped his pacing about the room. "Then how did it get down here?"

Charlotte darted a fearful look at Emily and sighed. It was time—probably long past time—to tell Anne and Papa about the intruder. They were as horrified as she'd feared they would be.

"I believe now that the intruder took it and gave it to Lucy Taylor, who brought it back here early yesterday morning to fool you. She sneaked in while you were still upstairs, after trapping me in a stone shed on the moors."

Her sisters gasped. While huddled close to the glowing fire, Charlotte explained what had happened and what she now believed to be true. It was exactly what Papa had feared, she realized. She had played detective and gotten so close to the truth that she'd become a threat.

"Come. We must tuck you into bed with a hot brick," Emily insisted, "before you contract pneumonia."

"I will change into dry clothes," Charlotte said, "but I must go and make sure Lucy—or Celia—and her accomplice are caught. I believe she nearly killed Mary Green. She was happy to leave me for dead on the moors. She may already have another victim in her sights." She threw off her blankets and stood. She swayed but grabbed the back of her chair. "I *must* stop her now."

20

Cabot Falls, Vermont
Present Day

Sofia went to get coffee for Officer Quimby and the rest of them, and she noticed her hands were shaking. *Good news and bad news*, she thought. *Which do I want to hear first?* If only she could ask for just the good news. She wanted to hear that Jim's name had been cleared, that he had his job back, and that her world was safe and secure again. She wasn't sure she could take more bad news right now.

The adults sat at the table, and the kids stood back in the doorway. Sofia thought of banishing them to their bedrooms, but they'd lived through it all with them. They had a right to hear firsthand what had happened.

"You were right, Mrs. Parker," the officer said, pulling a large envelope from inside his jacket. "This is what that self-addressed envelope contained."

The kids moved in closer after he dumped the contents on the table. He went through the items, one by one. There was a tan steno pad listing names that included some of the school's biggest stars in all four major sports. Next to the names were log-ins, passwords, Social Security numbers, student ID numbers for accessing their grades and accounts, and addresses.

Jim shook his head. "I can't believe this! It looks like organized crime!"

Officer Quimby agreed. "It isn't the mafia, but this crime is definitely organized." He poked through the other items. "It goes back three years. In addition to the information written in the notebook, there are USB thumb drives, a cellphone, some school assignments Mr. Jeffries hadn't completed yet, and several exams."

Luke reached over Sofia's shoulder. "Look how small this is!" He was right. The flash drives were tiny: retractable, mini swivel drives that would barely be noticeable when stuck in the back of the computers.

"That's how Adam captured usernames and passwords without the teachers noticing. He taught kids how to insert a USB device into certain teachers' computers so he could record the instructors' keystrokes." Officer Quimby gathered up the evidence and replaced it in the envelope. "Young Adam was in your classroom to retrieve one such flash drive when you surprised him."

"What now?" Jim asked.

"Mr. Jeffries has already been brought in for questioning. When he finally broke his silence—after a full day—he opened up with us about how they pulled it off, and why. He didn't have enough money from his retirement to care for his grandson, not now and not to send him to college. For some students, he did their work outright. For others, he provided homework answers so they could fill out the tests themselves. The tutor charged as much as forty-five dollars an hour for his services. His grandson is apparently the technical help, getting passwords and log-in information to change student grades and access the exams."

"He could really do that?" Matthew asked, eyes wide.

"Yes. To Mr. Jeffries's embarrassment, his grandson was quite happy to brag about it."

Wynter looked ready to cry. "So Mr. Jeffries is the one who made my science grade higher?" she asked. "But why? He didn't ask me for any money."

Officer Quimby spread his hands wide. "I don't know, Wynter. He may simply have really liked you and thought he was helping. Mr. Jeffries charged a hefty price to the rich students. He was shocked today to discover that his grandson was making double money from them on the side."

"What do you mean?" Sofia asked.

"After the grandfather helped them cheat for a price, the grandson followed up later. He had access to all the records, and he blackmailed students to keep quiet about it."

Just then, the phone rang. Luke answered it. "Dad? It's your principal."

Every voice fell silent as Jim went to the phone. "Hello, Ed." Sofia caught Vanessa's eye and winked as they all shamelessly eavesdropped. "No, I understand. You did what you had to do." Jim paused again. "Actually, a police officer just filled us in on the details. Quite a shock." This time there was a longer pause. "You don't need to do that. I'll just be glad to get back to teaching."

He hung up and returned to the table. "I guess you heard." He grinned. "That was Ed Piper, and it's all cleared up. He even offered to make a public apology."

Good, Sofia thought. She wanted everyone at the high school to hear the truth.

"The newspaper will also report that you were cleared," Officer Quimby said. He finished his cup of coffee, then rose. Patting Fergus on the head, he nodded to the kids and shook Jim's hand. Sofia walked with him to the door.

"I can't thank you enough," she said.

"No, I thank you for your help," he said. "Now I hope you can all put the whole mess behind you and get on with something more fun."

Sofia smiled. She could certainly agree, and she knew what it was going to be.

Yorkshire, England
July 1848

Within the hour, Charlotte had changed clothes and had a hot meal. Lucy's trail had probably grown cold already, but Charlotte had to try to find her.

Patrick Brontë was waiting when she came down the stairs. "I have been thinking, Daughter. You only need to go to Keighley. Demand that the constable there telegraph Inspector Tipp with what you have discovered. Then you come home."

"Oh, Papa, that would never work. Even if he believes me about Lucy locking me in the shed, he would think me mad if I claimed Lucy was Celia May and Celia May is the thief he is hunting." She paced from the front door to the staircase and back again. Finally, she stopped. "I have no choice. I have to go back to Leeds and see the inspector."

"Wait." Anne grabbed her arm. "What if he has gone back to London by now?"

Charlotte considered this. "Then I will continue on to London and force him to listen to me there."

Anne's face lost what little color she had. "Then I'm coming with you."

Charlotte knew she should argue with her delicate sister, but in truth, she would appreciate a companion on the trip.

Her silent, steady presence would give Charlotte moral support. "Yes, do come with me."

The rain had eased, so the walk to Keighley was warmer, although inches deep in mud in the low spots. By the time their train arrived in Leeds, Charlotte was acutely aware of how bruised she was after a night spent on the moors. But remembering her terror fortified her determination to find Lucy or Celia or whoever she was and make sure the inspector arrested her.

When they stopped in at the stationmaster's office, Inspector Tipp was there, sorting several piles of papers. He took one look at Charlotte, then snatched up his papers and shoved them into a leather case.

"You're still here!" Charlotte exclaimed.

He tipped his hat to both ladies. "If you'll excuse me, I am just on my way to London."

"But wait. I know who tried to kill Mary Green."

Inspector Tipp nodded. "As it happens, so do I, and he's been arrested." He tried to edge around Charlotte.

"Whom did you arrest?" Charlotte demanded, blocking his way.

The inspector closed his eyes and breathed heavily. "The guard, Nic Strada," he finally said. "It will be in the papers tomorrow."

"He's not your thief," Charlotte protested, "but I know who is. She tried to kill me yesterday."

"Kill you?"

"Well, she trapped me while she got away."

"Did you say *she*?" the inspector asked.

"Yes. It was Celia May, disguised as a writer named Lucy Taylor."

Charlotte waited, but Inspector Tipp made no response. Unless she was mistaken, he was trying hard not to laugh. When he finally spoke, he said, "Miss Brontë, as I have said more than once, I admire your ability as an author. But we have our guilty man, and I am going home."

He stepped around her, walked outside, and strolled to the first-class carriages on the platform servicing southbound trains.

Furious at being dismissed, Charlotte followed him. A porter with a mountain of luggage blocked her way, and as she stepped around him, she spotted a slender, clean-shaven guard stacking more luggage on the platform by the first-class carriages.

"Anne, look! Is that the guard who knocked you down?" Charlotte asked.

Anne frowned and stared at him. "Yes, I think it is," Anne whispered.

"Come on." As they approached, Charlotte watched the guard work. He struggled with the heavier bags. His hat was still too large, covering his hair and even the tops of his ears. He seemed to worry more about keeping his hat on than hoisting the luggage up. Charlotte marched up behind the guard, pulled off the oversize cap, and yanked out several pins. Long red hair tumbled down. "Hello, Celia," Charlotte said. "Or should I say Lucy?"

The guard whirled around and gave Charlotte a heavy push, but Charlotte grabbed one arm and Anne grabbed the other. "Inspector Tipp!" Charlotte shouted, keeping her grip on the struggling guard.

Now it all made sense. She recalled how this guard kept disappearing, and when James Thomas looked for Celia, she also disappeared and reappeared. She recalled Mr. Thomas spotting Celia sashaying from somewhere near the end of the train, fanning herself as she strolled along. Of course! Celia had been coming from the guard van, where she'd undoubtedly ducked inside to change clothes and switch disguises. And the way she always patted her blond hair in the back? It wasn't just vanity. She was checking to make sure her wig was in place.

This time, as Charlotte told her story back in the stationmaster's office, the inspector listened. "Celia might have changed in the lavatories," Charlotte concluded, "but she needed to stash her disguises and luggage somewhere. I think we should check the guard van."

They checked one guard van and came up empty. But in the second one, on a train that arrived from Liverpool, they found Celia's clothes and blond wig. Charlotte dug underneath the frilly dress and petticoats. "And look at this!" The severe black clothes, the ones that had reminded Charlotte of a riding habit, were there, along with the leather satchel that Lucy had carried.

Celia refused to speak. Even though she'd been caught red-handed, she didn't appear afraid or guilty. The inspector agreed that Celia probably had an accomplice. *And she's expecting to be rescued by him*, Charlotte realized.

Inspector Tipp cleared his throat, and he had the grace to look embarrassed. "Do you think Nic Strada is her accomplice?"

"No, I don't." Charlotte remembered discovering him, crying, after they believed Mary was dead. He had been experiencing genuine grief.

Anne spoke up for the first time. "When the intruder attacked Charlotte, our sister, Emily, helped her beat him off," she said. "I think I ripped his pocket. A note fell out that said 'Keep your guard up.' If he were the accomplice, could that be a hint to meet in the guard train?"

The inspector stroked the end of his beak-shaped nose. "That seems a little far-fetched," he said.

Charlotte jumped to her sister's defense. "I think Anne is onto something. If Celia is using her disguise as a guard to steal from those riding the trains, her accomplice will stick close by to take the stolen items from her. Meeting in the guard car would be the perfect cover. The accomplice could come to the guard car supposedly to collect his trunk." She waved a hand at the oversize luggage that was too heavy to be tossed up on top of the first-class carriages. "And Celia as a guard would have every right to be in here. I'm sure that when dressed as Celia May, she sweet-talks many gullible men out of their money or valuables. Feeling foolish, I bet that many of them are so embarrassed that they don't even report it."

Celia fluttered her eyelashes at Charlotte. "You are one jealous old spinster," she said. "I doubt if you could sweet-talk anyone. I feel quite sorry for you."

Before Charlotte could answer, Anne grabbed her sister's arm and laid a finger to her lips. She was watching out the van's rear window. As they waited in silence, footsteps halted outside the open van door. The inspector moved back out of sight, and Charlotte barely breathed.

"Hello? Might I come in?" called a cultured voice. When no one answered, a man in top hat and tails stepped into the guard van. Charlotte gaped openly at him. Although no longer dressed as a schoolmaster, the man was unquestionably George Hopkins.

He spotted Celia, looked startled at her long hair tumbled about the shoulders of her guard's uniform, and opened his mouth to speak. Celia gave a quick jerk of her head. George Hopkins swung around and spotted Inspector Tipp. Then his gaze took in the Brontë sisters as they emerged from the shadows.

"Did I interrupt something?" he finally said. "I want my trunk, but I can come back later." George Hopkins retreated back to the doorway.

Charlotte watched and waited. Did he wince when he twisted aside? Perhaps his leg still hurt after jumping from the trellis outside her window. "Wait," Charlotte said. "Did you hurt your leg? You seem to be favoring it."

His eyes narrowed, but then he smiled and shrugged. "New boots. One of them pinches." He hesitated. "Well, if that's all . . ."

"No, it's not," Inspector Tipp said. "I'm holding you for questioning in the attempted murder of Mary Green and the theft of her property."

"That's lunacy." He shook his head in disbelief. "You have no reason to detain me." He turned to leave.

Charlotte sprang forth and grabbed his coat sleeve and his hand. She shoved his sleeve up to reveal three deep fingernail scratches that were red and angry looking. "I knew I got you when you tried to smother me!"

Celia threw herself at Charlotte. "Get your hands off him!"

Inspector Tipp moved close behind Celia, threw his clasped hands over her head, and pinned her arms to her sides.

Within the hour, after questioning them both separately, Inspector Tipp had his case. George Hopkins and his wife, Celia May Hopkins, were arrested for Mary Green's attempted murder and theft of her possessions. Inspector Tipp also mentioned nearly a dozen other thefts on the rail line over the past year, and he expected to uncover even more. Among other techniques, Celia admitted to conning silly older men out of money and valuables after she laced their tea with a little laudanum.

The inspector also took Stationmaster Woodford in for questioning. He found it difficult to believe that a guard not hired by the railroad could operate under a stationmaster's jurisdiction without his awareness of it. In addition, George Hopkins was held on suspicion of pushing Charlotte in front of the train in London and trying to smother her in her own bed, two more counts of attempted murder.

"You'll never prove that was me." George Hopkins yawned with apparent boredom.

"Give me his boots, Inspector, the ones he's wearing and any in his trunk," Charlotte had replied. "I made two molds of his footprints where he jumped down into the mud. I still have one cast." She smiled with satisfaction as the color drained from the man's face. "They will match."

21

Yorkshire, England
July 1848

A week later, after Charlotte and Anne had fully recuperated from their ordeal, Charlotte was outside weeding the flower beds when the post arrived. She stood and stretched, admiring as always the letter carrier's red uniform. *No wonder they are called Robins*, she thought.

"Package for you today, Miss Brontë," he said, digging in his letter pouch.

Charlotte wiped the soil from her hands on her apron and reached for the soft package. It was too lumpy to be a book manuscript back from her publisher. Anyway, the return address was in Leeds. She carried it to the bench under the oak tree in the corner of the front garden.

She untied the string and saved the length in her apron pocket, then carefully unwrapped the brown paper. Inside was a letter, which she set aside, and a beautiful piece of embroidered lavender cloth. She shook it out, at once recognizing the fancy paisley shawl that Mary had worn the day they met.

Admiring it before refolding it, she laid it carefully on the brown paper, then tore open the envelope. Large, loopy writing covered two sheets of paper. *Such extravagance*, Charlotte thought automatically. But then, young Mary Green could probably afford to use as many sheets of stationery as she chose. Judging by the upward slant of the handwriting, she'd been optimistic when she penned the letter.

I am recovering well, Mary had written, *and my spirits are high, thanks to you.*

Charlotte smiled, and her pleasure increased the more she read. Mary was overjoyed with how events had turned out. Niccolo Strada had been escorted to the house by Inspector Tipp so that Mary could confirm his story about why he was in contact with her. The timing couldn't have been better. Her mother had still been in such a state of shock after Mary "came back from the dead," as she put it, that Isobel Green would have granted her daughter anything.

"I told Mama and Papa that only one thing would make me happy: permission for Nic to court me."

They'd granted it at once, and since then, they were astounded at Mary's rapid recovery. "I no longer require the London doctor's medicine either!"

Charlotte laid the letter down in her lap, grateful for that news especially. She was convinced that the laudanum had made her brother's illness worse, not better. She had no doubt that Mary would recover much better without it.

There was more on the second page. "The letters I told you about disappeared when I was unconscious. I no longer worry that Mama will discover my relationship with Nic, but I do wish I had my special letters back. They were a written history of the beginning of our love."

In that, at least, Charlotte could put Mary Green's mind at rest. She'd go indoors right away and write her a thank-you note for the shawl. She would add her note to the missing package of letters.

Three Years Later:
Yorkshire, England
1851

Charlotte was delighted when she saw Mary Green's handwriting on the envelope. *Not Mary Green,* she reminded herself. *Mary Strada.* She sighed, acknowledging that Mary Green had never been destined to be a spinster like Charlotte.

Charlotte's high spirits were soon deflated by the shocking news contained in the letter. Mary wrote that her parents had both died in a fire after their house was struck by lightning.

I hardly know what to think or feel, Mary wrote. *With no family now, Nic has persuaded me to move to his home in Florence, Italy, to be near his family. Florence has a big railroad station. He will get work there.*

Wiping her eyes, Charlotte stared out her bedroom window, remembering the loss of her own mother all those years ago. Her heart went out to Mary as she returned to her letter.

I want my son and daughter to have the love of a nonna in their lives. Niccolo's mama is beside herself with joy at our move to Italy. We leave on the train tomorrow and then set sail from Liverpool the day after. I will always remember you with affection.

"And I, you," Charlotte whispered, drawing the lavender paisley shawl more closely around her shoulders.

Three Years Later:
Yorkshire, England
Thursday, June 29, 1854

Charlotte stood before her mirror, adjusting the collar and sleeve cuffs edged in velvet. The simple style of her silver and dark mauve silk going-away dress was in keeping with her newly married status. She glanced at the clock. She'd been married at eight that morning in the St. Michael and All Angels Church, so she'd been Mrs. Arthur Bell Nicholls for six hours. He waited for her downstairs.

Charlotte's father had not felt well enough to attend her small wedding, but dear Nell had been there. If only Anne or Emily could have attended her wedding. Charlotte still missed her siblings dreadfully. Branwell and Emily had died in September and December of 1848, respectively, and Anne in the spring of 1849. Those were bleak years for her and Papa. Charlotte never would have guessed that she could be happy again.

After the honeymoon, she and her new husband would continue to live in the parsonage with her aging father. Arthur had served her father as assistant curate for many years, and it seemed fitting to Charlotte that he would live in the parsonage with them.

"Charlotte," Arthur called up the staircase. "We should leave now."

"Coming," she called back. She only needed to add one more thing to complete her outfit: the lavender paisley silk shawl she'd received as a gift from Mary Green six years ago. It was the nicest shawl she owned, and it set off her going-away dress perfectly.

Turning away from the mirror, she started down the stairs to begin her new life.

Cabot Falls, Vermont
Present Day

After Officer Quimby left and Sofia got the kids in bed, she was too wired to sleep. Long after Jim was snoring softly, she crept downstairs. She wouldn't be teaching at the high school anymore, so if she stayed up late working on her quilt history, it wouldn't matter.

And how wonderful to have her mind free to enjoy it now!

With a cup of spiced tea and a plate of crispy shortbread, she settled in for as long as she felt like working. She loved when the house was quiet and the phone didn't ring.

She dug out all of Marla's photocopies. She understood that Elizabeth Gaskell went to the city of Bronte after Charlotte's death, but why? Would the name of the castle being the same as her famous friend be enough for Gaskell to make that long voyage? And more importantly for Sofia, did it somehow point to an ancestor who'd pieced her lavender paisley silk square?

Sipping her tea, Sofia reread material Marla had copied from certain genealogy websites, and then she reviewed the websites devoted to the Brontës.

And it was there that she discovered what linked the Brontë family to the Italian island. Charlotte's father, Patrick, had been born Patrick Brunty. His hero at that time was Admiral Lord Nelson. Nelson had been made Duke of Bronte after helping a king return to the throne. Bronte was the name of an estate or castle in Sicily. So Charlotte's father chose the name Brontë based on the town in Sicily, the town that Elizabeth Gaskell visited after she wrote Charlotte's biography, *The Life of Charlotte Brontë*.

Still . . . it didn't point to Sofia's ancestor, the maker of the lavender paisley quilt square.

Next, Sofia browsed the online collection of the Brontë Parsonage Museum, once the home of the Brontë family. They had Charlotte's going-away outfit from the day of her wedding in 1854 to Arthur Bell Nicholls, a beautiful mauve dress, a light purple the color of the heather on the moors. A brief note under the dress said Charlotte also wore a lavender paisley shawl that day.

That shawl was given to a good friend the year after Charlotte's wedding, just before Charlotte died during her pregnancy.

Sofia's heartbeat quickened. *Who was this friend?* Was the friend of Charlotte's who ended up with the shawl the ancestor Sofia was hunting? She felt so very close to solving the puzzle of the eleventh quilt square, but she was still missing that one final definitive piece.

It was getting late—past two o'clock already—and she needed to wind down. But that didn't happen. Before shutting down her laptop, Sofia noticed an Internet link that included notes written by Elizabeth Gaskell, Charlotte's biographer and close friend, later in life. Clicking on the link, she discovered the answer to her quest at last.

Gaskell's notes concerned a visit to Italy she had taken as a type of pilgrimage for her dear friend. In Charlotte's honor, when visiting the town of Bronte in Sicily, she'd donated a signed copy of *Jane Eyre*.

But that wasn't the only place she visited in honor of her friend. She'd come home to England after visiting Florence to return Charlotte's lavender paisley silk shawl to its rightful owner.

Sofia was wide awake now. Something in her sensed that she was about to meet the woman who contributed the eleventh quilt square.

In 1848, Gaskell wrote, *Charlotte and Anne had gone to London to reveal their true identities to their publisher. On the way home on their train, a young acquaintance, Mary Green of Leeds, was attacked and nearly died. Thanks to Charlotte's determination and detection, a married couple was arrested for this crime and many others. In gratitude, Mary gave a lavender paisley shawl to Charlotte. Mary and Charlotte became close friends and visited each other through the years. In 1851, Mary's parents died, and she and her husband, son, and daughter moved to Florence, Italy, to live near the family of her husband, Niccolo Strada. In 1855, as Charlotte lay dying in the parsonage she had long called home—in the moors where she once said summer never comes—she asked me to mail the shawl to Mary so that she could hand it down to her own daughter one day. Instead, I made the journey to Italy, first to Bronte, Sicily, and later to Florence. I met with Mary in Florence and gave her the shawl in person. She promised to keep the shawl for her daughter and would tell her someday how, for seven years, her shawl had belonged to one of the greatest British writers ever born. Charlotte would have liked that.*

Yes, Sofia thought, *Charlotte would have liked that.* So Mary Green Strada was Sofia's ancestor, but the lavender silk shawl had also belonged to Charlotte Brontë. Sofia could hardly wrap her mind around it.

Sofia loved that Mary's children got to grow up loving and knowing their Italian *nonna,* just as Sofia had. She thought longingly of Nonna now, wishing she could talk to her and share her excitement at this discovery. Sofia longed to walk in Charlotte's and Mary's footsteps and leave a legacy that would last.

There in the early morning hours, Sofia seemed to sense Nonna whispering in her ear. "You have already left a legacy, *mia nipotina.* It is found upstairs in the hearts of that wonderful, peaceful family."

Family. Love. Loyalty. Her lasting legacy.

Learn more about Annie's fiction books at

AnniesFiction.com

- Access your e-books
- Discover exciting new series
- Read sample chapters
- Watch video book trailers
- Share your feedback

We've designed the Annie's Fiction website especially for you!

Plus, manage your account online!

- Check your account status
- Make payments online
- Update your address

ANNIE'S ATTIC
MYSTERIES®

CREATIVE WOMAN
MYSTERIES®

Annie's
Quilted
Mysteries™

Annie's
Mysteries
Unraveled™

ANNIE'S
SECRETS
of the QUILT™

AMISH
INN
MYSTERIES™

Visit us at AnniesFiction.com